Conrad stared, fascinated, at the screens. He saw monstrous serpentine shapes, threshing about on the perimeter. A beam of light caught one as it reared, showing the glistening, fantastic, and segmented body.

The face—if you could call it that—was fully two meters in diameter. The mouth, wide open, was a black chasm, large enough to take in four men side by side. The seven eyes—if they were eyes—were spaced at regular intervals in a half-moon shape close over the thick, top, obscene lip of the cavernous mouth. They reflected the searchlight beam, shining briefly like grotesque stars.

Conrad wiped the sweat from his forehead.

"Ladies and gents," he said, as calmly as he could, "we have now discovered the nature of the opposition."

Fawcett Gold Medal Books
by Richard Avery:

THE EXPENDABLES

#1 THE DEATHWORMS OF KRATOS

#2 THE RINGS OF TANTALUS

The Expendables #1

The Deathworms of Kratos

Richard Avery

A FAWCETT GOLD MEDAL BOOK

Fawcett Publications, Inc., Greenwich, Connecticut

THE EXPENDABLES #1

THE DEATHWORMS OF KRATOS

Copyright © 1974 by Richard Avery

Printed in the United States of America

First printing: October 1975

1 2 3 4 5 6 7 8 9 10

The Deathworms of Kratos

Rendezvous with Kratos

EVENT ONE

Command Alert

The robot was man-sized, but there was nothing human in its appearance. It was just a highly efficient, highly complex machine with a synthetic identity encoded in its electronic brain. It had the word Matthew painted on its chest plate and on its back plate.

It bent over the unconscious body on the intensive care bench in the resuscitation chamber and gently massaged, working on key areas according to a procedure that had been carefully programmed into its memory circuits. The robot wore thermal gloves so that its steel fingers would not damage the pale, cold flesh and so that the radiant heat would go where it was most needed. Simultaneously, the robot monitored the minute changes of body temperature, the weak but increasing heart-beat, the slow climb in blood pressure.

Gentle, rhythmic pressure on the chest had triggered the breathing cycle. The unconscious man gave a faint, involuntary groan. The robot noted with approval. A toe twitched, then a finger. What had been almost dead was fighting its way back to life.

Most of the resuscitation procedure had been automatic. On computer instruction, the body had been ejected from its low-temperature casket and subjected to measured doses of infra-red radiation at decreasing intervals before being transferred to the intensive care unit where, in controlled sequence, normal life-functions would be restored. The rest now was up to the I.C. monitoring equipment and the decisions of the robot.

The naked man groaned once more. His heart-beat strengthened. His eye-lids fluttered. The robot altered its pattern of massage. Presently, it removed the thermal gloves and placed a mask over the man's nose and mouth. Oxygen-enriched air was pumped into the lungs in pulses synchronous with the weak breathing cycle.

In less than a minute, the man was conscious. He opened his eyes and cried out in anguish. The robot knew why he cried out. The vision analysis centres of the brain were receiving conflicting signals. Deftly, the robot placed a silver patch over one eye. The man gave a sigh and relaxed. He focused his uncovered eye on the robot, staring at it fixedly. The robot took away the mask. Breathing was almost normal.

"Sir," said the robot, "do you hear me clearly?"

"I hear you clearly."

"Do you experience any pain?"

"No, but I feel very tired."

"Are you in a condition to receive data?"

The man smiled faintly. "I am in a condition to receive data."

"Sir, you have been in suspended animation for approximately five hundred and forty hours, Standard Earth Time. About eighty-five per cent of suspended

animation subjects suffer temporary amnesia upon resuscitation. I am therefore empowered to remind you
of key data. You are James Conrad, commander of the
faster-than-light vessel *Santa Maria*. The vessel is now
in stable orbit round the planet Altair Four, designated
as Kratos by the Extra-Solar Planets Evaluating and
Normalising Department of the United Nations. Your
mission is to prove Kratos fit for human colonisation.
Your personnel consist of six human beings, designated
as Expendables, and six self programming robots, type
S.P.9. I am S.P.9/1, designated as Matthew for your
convenience. I have command circuits that can override the independent circuitry of the other five robots. I
am programmed to obey any lawful command you
give. Do you understand me?"

The naked man sighed. "I understand you but, as
yet, I do not fully remember. How long will it be before
I get normal recall?"

"Normally, sir, it would not be longer than 1.5 hours
S.E.T. Your responses have been good, therefore I
would anticipate that normal recall would occur well
within that time limit."

Conrad shivered. "I feel bloody cold."

"I am sorry, sir. I am not empowered to vary the
temperature programme. But presently you should feel
comfortable."

"What the hell is this business about lawful commands?" demanded Conrad irritably. "Can I command
you or can I not?"

"You can command me, sir, in any way that does
not involve the Asimov Inhibition."

"What the hell is that?"

"You command me in any way that does not involve

harming, putting at risk, or causing the death of another human being."

"That seems reasonable."

"Yes, sir."

"Have we any brandy aboard the *Santa Maria*?"

"Yes, sir. There are twenty-eight litres of brandy, designated as Hennessy XO in Number One hold. There are also supplies of several alcoholic beverages, including seventy-seven litres of—"

"Get me a large brandy, Matthew, and shut up."

"It is not advisable at this stage, sir."

James Conrad sat up. It hurt him considerably, but he made it. "Get the bloody brandy, damn you. And do it quick. I am now in command."

"Yes, sir."

Conrad let out a great cry.

"You experience pain, sir?"

"No, Matthew. I'm beginning to remember. Now hurry with that brandy, damn you!"

FLASH ONE

Court-Martial

The man with the bandage round his head, covering one eye, stood stiffly at attention, his uniform cap under his arm. According to drill regulations it was the wrong arm. But then he only had one arm. So drill procedure had to be modified. The empty right sleeve was tucked neatly into the pocket of his dress uniform. The four gold bars visible near the end of the other sleeve showed that he was a captain in the United Nations Space Service.

With his one good eye, he stared ahead impassively in best regulation fashion, focusing on no one, on nothing. It was his function not to observe, only to hear. Only to hear the words that would inevitably destroy his future, everything he had ever wanted. Like every other man, he had often wondered what it was like to die. Now he was beginning to understand. Because this was a kind of dying.

He was standing facing a dais and a long table behind which five men sat. They were all members of the U.N.S.S. One was a commander, two were captains, one was a commodore; and the president of the court martial was a full admiral.

The chamber was one of the most dramatic structures on Luna. It was a huge transparent dome of double-panelled plastiglass. The panels were set in an intricate tracery of steel frames, spreading out from the apex of the dome like a spider's web. The plastiglass was almost as tough as steel and lighter than titanium. It was also phototropic. During the long lunar day (fourteen Earth days) it turned milky, opaque, reflecting the harsh radiation of the sun, unfiltered by any atmosphere. During the equally long lunar night, it became transparent once again, revealing the magnificent wilderness of stars. That was why it was called the Star Chamber.

Captain James Conrad, D.S.S.C. and bar (only seventeen serving captains had been awarded the Distinguished Space Service Cross, and only nine had received the additional distinction of the silver bar) was mildly surprised at his own lack of emotion. He already knew what the verdict of the court-martial would be—what it must be if service discipline were to be maintained. And yet he felt no shame, not even fear. Only regret. He had gambled, and the gamble had not succeeded. One must pay one's debts.

The president of the court-martial rose.

"Captain Conrad, by the authority vested in me by the United Nations Space Command, Department of Solar Patrol, Moscow, Earth, I have convened this court-martial to examine the evidence supporting the three charges brought against you by Commodore Erwin G. Streffens, officer commanding Lunar Squadron. Under the articles of space service, it is my duty to ask you for the final time if you still recognise the validity of this court. I have to advise you that if your answer is negative, you will retain the right of appeal. However, if your answer is affirmative, the findings of this tribunal will be irreversible. Captain Conrad, do you still recognise the validity of this court?"

"Affirmative, sir."

What was the point in asking for a playback? The evidence would still be the same, the verdict would still be the same. If you are going to get the chop, Conrad thought, there is no point in getting it twice.

"Your answer, Captain Conrad, has now been entered in the record. Before delivering the verdicts arrived at by a majority vote taken by my brother officers and myself, I must again ask you if you challenge any of the evidence brought either by the prosecuting officer or the defending officer. If you so do, such evidence may yet be re-examined and may affect the judgment delivered by this court-martial. Do you so challenge?"

"Negative, sir."

The facts had been presented fairly—and the facts could not be denied. And hell, you couldn't challenge on the grounds that fate had been a trifle unkind. But Conrad's curiosity was suddenly aroused. The president had said a majority vote not a unanimous one. Who had been the officer—or even officers—who had tried to exercise charity? Probably one or both of the captains. They, at least, would understand how he had felt. But he would never know who had tried to be kind.

The president was speaking once more. "Finally, Captain Conrad, I have to ask if you have any reason to believe that any officer appointed to serve in any capacity at this court-martial may have harboured any personal animosity towards you either before or during these proceedings."

"Negative, sir."

Streffens had never liked him, but then he had never liked Streffens. The commodore was a desk man, a career officer who seemed to think that bits of paper, regulations and drill manuals were more important than men. Conrad himself was a spaceman—first, last and always. Streffens may have been waiting for just such an opportunity. Not that it mattered. Conrad had wilfully disobeyed the lawful and reasonable orders of his superior officer. That was what counted. The rest was catastrophe.

President Admiral Kotuzov cleared his throat noisily and lifted a couple of papers from the table. He adjusted his old-fashioned spectacles and read the findings with a clear, unhesitating voice.

"Captain Conrad, the three charges brought against you are as follows. One, that you wilfully and repeatedly disobeyed the orders of your commanding officer. Two, that in doing so you put at risk the safety of the vessel *S.S. Gagarin* then under your command. Three, that the result of your subsequent actions brought about the unnecessary deaths of three of your crew members and one engineer officer.

"The established facts are as follows. At 0352 G.M.T. on the thirteenth day of August in the year 2071 the vessel *S.S. Einstein* lifted from Mercury with a cargo of ingot platinum and other rare metals, bound for Mars. Unfortunately the reaction system failed before the second power manoeuvre could be completed leaving the vessel in a rapidly decaying solar orbit. The late Captain Brandt reported his position, estimating that in less than ninety hours the *Einstein* would fall into the solar danger zone. The information was relayed on distress channel to O.C. Lunar Squadron. The nearest vessel to the *Einstein* was your own, then returning from low-orbit survey of Venus. Computer extrapolations revealed that with maximum use of power manoeuvres, you were at least one hundred and five hours from a theoretical rendezvous point with the doomed vessel."

Admiral Kotuzov cleared his throat once more.

"At 0519 G.M.T. you signalled O.C. Lunar Squadron requesting permission to attempt rendezvous. Permission was denied. You then signalled your intention to attempt rendezvous. Again, permission was denied and you were commanded to return to Luna. You then cut off communication with O.C. Lunar Squadron and proceeded with your intention.

"As a result, the *Gagarin* made rendezvous with the *Einstein* three hours after it had already passed into the danger zone. It is unfortunate and, perhaps, unlucky for you that this occurred during a period of intense solar activity. The radiation hazards were already unacceptable. It is to your credit that you succeeded in transferring two of the personnel of the stricken vessel. It is to your discredit that four of your own crew perished as a result and that you yourself were gravely injured. That the two you rescued also subsequently died as a result of irradiation emphasises the folly of your disobedience. I would remind you that the successful operation of the United Nations Space Service cannot be founded on Quixotic gestures, however commendable the motivation might be. Discipline is necessary at all times if man is to extend his dominion in space.

"It is the finding of this court-martial that, on the first count, you are guilty as charged. On the second count, you are found to be not guilty, since the safety of the *S.S. Gagarin* could only have been at risk if, as a result of your actions, insufficient engineering staff survived to carry out the necessary power manoeuvres to escape from the danger zone. On the third count, you are found to be guilty."

Again Kotuzov cleared his throat noisily.

"Therefore, the sentence of this court is that you shall be reduced to the rank of commander and that you shall forfeit ten years' seniority. Further, that before you are again offered an independent command, you will undergo psychiatric examination to determine your ability to respond to orders."

It was better than Conrad had hoped. But it was still the death knell. Who, in his right mind, would ever entrust a ship to a man who would not obey orders? Conrad could see long years ahead being somebody's Number One—If he were lucky. But how many captains would want to take on someone who was once their equal and for whom they could only feel pity? Further, how many would want an Exec who had been court-martialled for disobeying orders? Conrad revised his appreciation. All he could see in the immediate future was an indeterminate period of leave on Terra at half-pay. Maybe someone would be kind enough to let him lecture on astronautics at some obscure space academy in the American Mid-West.

Suddenly, he was aware that Admiral Kotuzov had sat down, and that everyone seemed to be staring at him.

He funbled awkwardly with his cap, managed somehow to get it back on his head, and saluted as smartly as he could with the wrong arm.

"Sir! Thank you, sir," he said in a clear even voice. Then like an automaton, with all eyes upon him, he marched stiffly from the Star Chamber.

In the antechamber, the gentlemen of the media waited like a pack of hungry wolves. They surrounded him, almost engulfed him.

"Captain Conrad, did you get a fair trial?"

"Affirmative. Incidentally, I am now improperly dressed, having been reduced to the rank of commander."

"Will you appeal, sir?"

"Negative."

"Millions of people on Terra are with you, captain —er—commander. Do you know that a petition with approximately five million signatures from people of all nations will be presented on your behalf to the Secretary-General?"

"I did not know, and I do not want to know. Allow me to pass, please. As far as I am concerned, the incident is now closed. You will do me a big favour by leaving it that way."

"Captain, would you consent to being nominated for political—"

Conrad lost his patience. "Gentlemen, I am tired. I wish to relax. Will you kindly let me pass?"

"Commander, is it true that you have a feud with Commodore Streffens, and that—"

"Excuse me, I wish to pass."

But they would not let him pass, because he was to-day's news. And the babel of questions came thick and heavy. The vid men formed an apparently impenetrable barrier.

James Conrad raised his arm. "I intend to leave this place, and I do not wish any of you to follow me. Is that clear?"

"Sir, one final question. It has been rumoured that a woman was the cause of your hostility to Commodore Streffens. Will you confirm that—"

Conrad chopped expertly. The man went down gurgling. Some of the media men went to help him. A couple of brave ones still confronted Conrad.

"There is a report that you are psychiatrically unstable. Would you care to comment?"

Conrad struck again.

The last man to bar his path said insolently: "This interview is going out live, Commander. I hope you are aware of that."

A black rage gripped Conrad. "I am aware, my friend, that you are a vulture and, as such, somewhat obscene. Stand aside."

The man did not budge. "Do you realy wish to alienate—"

Expertly, Conrad kicked at his stomach then, as the man fell, smashed the edge of his hand on the back of the neck.

There were gasps and cries. Everyone drew back.

"I am glad you have finally got the message, gentlemen," said Conrad calmly. Bleakly, he realized that this little performance had destroyed his space career for good. He had publicly proved himself to be psychiatrically unstable. No one in his right mind would ever let James Conrad anywhere near a space ship again.

There was a brief silence. The media men made a pathway for him.

"I'll see you are broken for this!" snarled someone.

Conrad did not even bother to look who it was. He gave a grim smile. "There is nothing more you can do to me." He walked slowly out of the ante-chamber.

He badly needed a drink. Should he go to his room at Squadron Control and send out for a bottle and sit on his bed and get smashed and feel sorry for himself? No, by God! They would think he was hiding, that he had taken a beating and had crept away to lick his wounds. Let them all see—the ubiquitous them—that James Conrad, Commander U.N.S.S. ret (he determined to write his letter of resignation before he hit the booze) was not ashamed of himself. Or, at least, not ashamed of his attempt to take off the crew of the *Einstein*.

Later, as he sat at a table at the Jupiter Bar—the most fashionable rendezvous in Luna City—he began to regret his decision. The bar was crowded, but the seats at the tables near to his were vacant. He had a half empty of 140 proof Polish White Spirit in front of him. He didn't have to call for ice or tonic water. Whenever he needed them, they were delivered unobtrusively. The waiter who delivered them looked as if he were approaching an A-bomb with a short time trigger.

Conrad sipped his eighth drink and smiled to himself. He was aware that many eyes followed his every movement. He realised that the management was hoping he would pass out quietly without attempting to wreck the joint. He had no intention of becoming violent—but let them enjoy their suspense.

Somebody approached him. Brave fellow!

"Captain Conrad, may I have a word with you?"

By that time, Conrad wasn't focusing too well. But he could still register the cut of the clothes. Goddamned civilian!

"Haven't they told you. I'm a bogyman. Go away."

"I also am a bogyman, Captain Conrad. And I do not wish to go away."

"I'm a commander now, stupidhead."

"O.K. Commander."

"Ex-Commander."

"O.K. Ex-Commander."

"If you operate for the media, I'll probably bust your ribs. I have a good track record."

"I don't work for the media, and if you try to bust my ribs I'll break your one good arm for starters."

Conrad laughed. "So, we understand each other. Have a drink."

"Fine. I like Polish White Spirit. It saves a lot of time."

"Right." Another glass appeared miraculously. Conrad filled it with White Spirit, but he did not add any tonic. "I'm ahead. Catch up. Then tell me what you want."

The civilian downed his drink in one. Conrad raised an eyebrow. "You are going to regret that, my friend."

The civilian grinned. "Possibly. But I am playing for high stakes. My name is John Doe—no, really, it is—of the Extra Solar Commission. Conrad, how would you like a new start?"

"A new start in what, funny man?"

"Deep-space exploration. Your own command. Absolute authority."

"I still think I can break your ribs before you get my arm."

John Doe shrugged. "Let us hope it doesn't come to the test. I'm serious . . . Face it, Conrad. As of now you are expendable. We need expendable people. Talented people. That means you."

"For what?"

"Planet-proving. A very hazardous business. We don't have any reliable statistics yet on the mortality rate, but I think they may be high."

"Keep talking, Mr. John Doe. And, for your health's sake, pray that you interest me."

EVENT TWO

Sleeping Beauty

Conrad felt good. He had been out of suspended animation for more than six hours. Now he was no longer physically dependent on a computer-controlled programme or the efficiency of six robots. He was in command of the *Santa Maria* once more. And, as a good commander, his first duty was to see to the safety of his ship. He was almost disappointed to find that vessel and cargo were in virtually perfect condition. The only damage was what he had been briefed to expect. Pressure meters revealed some distortion of the emergence shield. He had been warned that when the ship emerged from sub-space, there would be a moment— less than a millionth of a second—when the "impact" of normal space produced tremendous stress. Conrad, who had a master's degree in astrophysics, could not understand how the emerging of a body into almost perfect vacuum could produce stress. But the mathematicians of ExPEND had given him a going-over; and he came out of it dazed, unconvinced, but resigned. He was mildly annoyed to discover that the mathematicians had been proved right.

As he proceeded on his tour of inspection, memories came back to him thick, fast, heavy. Sometimes like ever-changing patterns in a kaleidoscope. The psychologists had warned him that, even under suspended animation, he would not completely escape the trauma of Faster Than Light drive, or the sub-space jump, as the younger scientists called it.

He was irritated to find that the psychologists had also been dead right. As he inspected the ship, he was able to concentrate fully on the tasks before him. But, on another level, his mind was piecing together fragments of memory as a man might put together the pieces of a jig-saw puzzle. The psychologists had warned him that total recall was impossible. Something would always be lost under extreme trauma. Probably they were right there, too. But the torrent of memories was vivid—as if, somehow, Conrad were desperately asserting his own identity . . . I remember, therefore I am me . . .

He lined the robots up and inspected them. Matthew, Mark, Luke, John, Peter and Paul. Since Matthew had command circuits, Conrad made him put the others through basic reflex and response tests. They all functioned perfectly.

"Sir, do you wish now to proceed with the resuscitation programme?" suggested Matthew.

Conrad thought about it carefully. The shock of coming out of suspended animation in an orbiting ship was bad enough for a trained spaceman who was used to having to walk on bond-fuzz carpeting in a field of zero gravity. How much worse would it be for groundlings who would have to learn many new tricks? Besides, he still felt weak himself. Too weak as yet to cope with much in the way of abnormal reactions.

"We will resuscitate Lieutenant Smith only, for the present," he said at last. "If she reacts well, we will proceed with the others when she has recovered her strength—and memory."

"Decision noted. Shall I enter it in the log, sir?"

"Dammit, I am commander of this vessel, and I write my own log," snapped Conrad irritably.

"Yes, sir. Decision noted. Resuscitation of Lieutenant Smith will now begin. Will you rest until she is conscious?"

"No. She will need to see a human face when she comes out of S.A. I will be present for the entire procedure . . . My god, I'm hungry. Can any of you bloody machines knock up eggs and bacon?"

"Query, sir. Please define the term 'knock up'."

"Cook, damn you . . . I'm sorry. I'm tired."

"We are all multi-programmed," said Matthew. "I regret that our responses to idiomatic use of language are imperfect. All of us can prepare hot or cold food. In what condition do you wish the eggs to be and how many do you desire?"

"Two, soft."

"And the bacon, sir?"

Conrad remained irritable. "Bacon, rashers, three, crisp, hot—execute. Coffee, hot, black, sweet. One half litre—execute."

Matthew said: "Decision noted. Mark will execute. Where and when do you wish this food to be delivered, Commander?"

"To the resuscitation chamber, fifteen minutes from now. Execute."

"Decision noted, Commander."

"Let's go," said Conrad. "I want Lieutenant Smith brought out of S.A. with minimum trauma. You read me?"

"Request noted, sir," said Matthew imperturbably. "Optimum techniques will be applied."

Lieutenant Indira Smith looked very small and fragile as Matthew, wearing the thermal gloves, gently massaged the pallid flesh. Small, naked, defenceless . . . Like a drowned child . . .

Because her body was still very cold, Conrad could see clearly the joining of living thighs to prosthetic legs. The legs were a miracle of engineering, limb design and brilliant surgery. He hoped she would learn not to resent them too much. The fingers of his own prosthetic arm twitched as he became self-consciously aware of its existence . . .

Matthew began to massage close under her breast. With his other hand, he gripped the small fleshy bulge near the nipple in what seemed to be a strangely crude fashion. Conrad suppressed an immediate sense of outrage, realising that Matthew was only bringing heat and expert massage close to the heart. The robot was totally indifferent to the female body of Indira Smith.

Looking at the compact form, slack now yet still extraordinary graceful, Conrad wondered once more if he had been wise to choose a woman as his second-in-command. True, Surgeon Lieutenant Indira Smith had already demonstrated her physical toughness; but could she be mentally tough also? In the event of his death or incapacitation, would she be strong enough to assert her authority, command the loyalty of the team, and carry out the proving programme? He wished there had been time to get to know her better, to break through the barrier that had been set as a result of her horrific experiences in Brazil.

But, apart from that complication, women, in Conrad's experience, were vastly different from men in their emotional and intellectual responses. Their logic was different, they played by different rules, they accepted different values. Trying to anticipate a woman's reaction to any given situation, he thought cynically, was like playing Russian roulette. You pressed the trigger, never knowing if the gun was going to go bang or click.

Maybe he should have got her to bed—drunk or sober—before he recruited her for the Expendables. In bed, he reflected, women are always more naked than men. He would have discovered much . . . But, in view of the Brazilian episode, that would have been a tough proposition. A very tough proposition. Besides, there just hadn't been the time.

So now, here he was, committed to the proving of Kratos with a second-in-command, who might or might not flip her lid at the first real crisis. Big deal! He realised it had been unfair to push her into a position of such responsibility. Silently, he cursed his own impulsiveness.

"How goes it, Matthew?"

"Temperature is still several degrees below independent life-support, Commander. I record intermittent heart response. The breathing cycle is still unactivated. Condition normal for this stage."

Conrad glanced once more at Indira's blank face and began to pace up and down.

"You have been at it now for over one and a half hours. How much longer?"

"Resuscitation procedure is being carried out at normal pace. Satisfactory resuscitation may take between one hundred and one hundred and eighty minutes, depending on mass of subject and physical condition. Procedure should not be accelerated except in case of emergency. Query. Is the situation now designated as an emergency, Commander?"

"No, blast you. I'm sorry, Matthew."

Without interrupting his movement, Matthew said: "Query. What are you sorry for, Commander,"

Conrad was annoyed with himself. He should have known it was futile to apologise to a robot. "Cancel statement. Continue normal procedure."

Presently, the breathing cycle began. The compact breasts rose slightly, seemed to assume a flicker of independent life. Matthew opened the woman's mouth gently, then applied the oxygen mask. The responses strengthened. Her eyelids flickered, opened. Her eyes rolled vaguely, then the lids came down once more. Her breasts heaved and she groaned deeply—a muted cry of outrage.

Presently, her eyes opened and stayed open. She began to focus. She tried to move, and exhausted herself with the effort. She groaned once more.

She saw a body bending over her. She tried to focus on the face. She saw it was a man's face, and did not recognise it. There was something covering one of the eyes. It seemed to shine malevolently.

She shivered, and screamed.

Somebody, or *something,* she could not see, said in a

cold metallic voice: "Lieutenant Smith is responding normally, sir. Shall I begin the primary briefing?"

"No, I'll do that." It was the sinister-looking man bending over her who was speaking.

And then Indira Smith began the painful process of recall.

FLASH TWO

The Man with the Silver Patch

Surgeon Lieutenant Indira Smith, late of the Terran Disaster Corps, was feeling distinctly nervous. She was sitting on the edge of her chair in a small room in the offices of the Extra-Solar Planets Evaluating and Normalising Department (ExPEND), which was part of a U.N. project of which, until recently, she had never heard.

She had seen the ad while she was recovering from an abortive suicide bid. Her psychiatrist claimed she hadn't really wanted to commit suicide, only to call attention to her predicament. She was inclined to agree with him. As a surgeon she ought to have known how to cut her own wrists efficiently. But, then, not too many surgeons try to operate with nail scissors when they are three parts drunk.

The ad was interesting. It said simply: Is your I.Q. high? Are you in good health? Have you one or more special skills? If you are bored with dear old Earth, if an end game in the geriatrics ward doesn't grab you, if you have no family ties or connections, call us. Maybe we can make life interesting.

Indira had called the number given. A robosec questioned her, checked her Id, recorded her personal details and directed her to attend a London test centre for something called Universal Enterprises. At the test centre, she had been given an intensive physical examination. Then a psych team had grilled her for four hours. Then she had been given intelligence and initiative tests. Finally, she had been routed to this little office on the 140th floor of Park Lane Tower.

It was only then that she learned the name of the U.N. department that had run the ad. She was not much wiser. As far as Indira Smith knew, no extrasolar planets had yet been discovered. The title seemed meaningless.

As she waited patiently for the interview that would decide her future—if any—she felt a ghost pain in her left thigh. She knew it was not real; but it felt bloody real. Real enough to make her surreptitiously swallow an analgesic tablet when the girl behind the desk wasn't looking. Real enough to give her the hundredth total recall of horror. She felt the sweat break out on her forehead. The cold sweat of absolute fear.

She had been taking part—a very small part—in the Amazonia rehabilitation project. Countless small primitive tribes were having to be catapulted quickly into the twenty-first century because of Earth's voracious demand for energy and minerals. She had been working with Captain Ricardo Behar—the man she had hoped to marry one day—in an isolated Indian community when the bandits struck. They called themselves guerillas, rebels, freedom fighters, and other high-sounding titles. But they were just a bunch of sub-human sadists out for kicks. They made Ricardo watch while they raped her. Twenty of them, perhaps thirty. After the first three or four, she was beyond counting.

When they had finished, they gouged out Ricardo's eyes. She could still hear the way he screamed. Then they made her chew something that would deaden all feeling. Then they bound leather thongs tightly round her thighs and cut off her legs. She watched them dully, not feeling anything. They laughed and joked, talking about the U.N. woman who would now no longer be desirable to any man. Then they threw her legs into the river.

Mercifully—or was it mercifully?— a U.N. chopper came in before she could die of infection, trauma and the returning agony. She hadn't tried to commit suicide until nearly a year later, when the controls of a pair of perfect prosthetic legs had been wired perfectly into her nervous system, and she was ready to be discharged from hospital. The limbs were wonderful things of titanium and steel, powered by tiny atomic motors and covered in skin-tinted plastic that was barely distinguishable from living flesh. They were superb legs. They would run all day if she told them to. They could kick a hole in a concrete wall or enable her to move across a tennis court in a blur of co-ordinated action. But they weren't a woman's legs, they were only bi-integrated machines. That is why she got drunk and had a go with the nail scissors.

It might not have been too bad if Ricardo had survived. At least they could have shared their misfortune and perhaps have tried to make a life together. But Ricardo had been unable to bear what he had seen and endured. He had retreated into insanity. Finally, he had managed to briefly elude his nurses and had hurled himself through a seventh storey window.

So now, here she was, waiting to see if she was good enough for an unspecified job on a project of which she knew next to nothing. Big deal. Fatalistically, she already anticipated the verdict. She would be turned down. Who in his right mind would offer any responsible post to a failed suicide? The man in the next room would have on his desk her psychofile, medical reports, career summary and Id date. If he had any sense, he would already know that she was unstable and therefore not to be trusted. No matter. Next time the do-it-yourself surgery would be more efficient . . .

Despite the analgesic, the phantom pain still nagged at her. She popped another tablet into her mouth just as the secretary said: "The commander will see you now, Lieutenant Smith. Please go in." The secretary gestured towards the door leading to the inner sanctum.

The room was sparsely furnished. Apart from the communications console and computer terminal, there was only a large desk and a couple of chairs. Sitting behind the desk was a man who wore a silver patch over one eye. He rose as she entered, and extended his hand across the desk.

"Please sit down, Lieutenant Smith. I am James Conrad."

She shook hands, noting the cool hardness of his fingers, and sat down. Suddenly, she recognised his face.

"Thank you, Commander Conrad."

"May I offer you a drink, a cigarette?"

"A drink, yes. A cigarette, no."

"Gin, vodka, whisky? I'm afraid I only have the hard stuff."

"Vodka and tonic, please."

Later she would regret the booze on top of the analgesics. But what the hell.

"The same for me, then," said Conrad.

He opened a drawer in his desk, took out bottles and glasses, poured the drinks.

"I believe you are Anglo-Indian, Lieutenant. A great combination. I once had an Anglo-Indian first officer who was the most attractive man—as far as women were concerned—in the system. He was also a demonic chess player. I never won a game."

"Actually," said Indira, "it's the other way round." She smiled. "As a result of the British Raj, Smith became a fine old Indian name. It is my mother who was English."

Conrad looked slightly puzzled. "According to your file, you should have black hair. Why is it white?"

"The file should have been updated," said Indira calmly. "I was raped by an unknown quantity of Brazilian Indians, then my lover's eyes were gouged out and my legs were cut off. Is that sufficient explanation?"

"It seems reasonable," said Conrad. "Do you know much about the kind of outfit you have applied to join?"

"No." The vodka and the analgesics were beginning to get together. "But perhaps we are wasting your time and mine. Can you really use a woman with tin legs, a failed suicide with a five-star hang-up about sex?"

He didn't answer her at once. He studied her objectively. She seemed almost frail, unsure of herself. When she had lifted the glass of vodka and tonic, her hand had been shaking. But he knew from her record that she was physically tough, had a high intelligence and had achieved much during her service with the Terran Disaster Corps. Her recent experiences would have been sufficient to totally destroy any ordinary woman. Indira Smith had come close to destruction, but the important fact was that she had survived. Somehow . . . And that was the vital factor.

He felt sorry for her; but he knew that he must not allow it to show. If he did, she would swallow the pity like she swallowed the vodka. And then she would feel even more sorry for herself. Someday, perhaps, he would be able to allow himself the luxury of telling her that he thought she was one hell of a woman. But not now. Now, the only thing to be determined was whether she was expendable.

He checked an impulse to smile, an impulse to touch her, an impulse to try to reassure her.

"Excuse my lack of sympathy," said Conrad coldly, "but I just may be able to use a woman with tin legs etcetera. Do you want to hear about the job?"

She sighed. "If it is your pleasure, and if it will brighten a dull afternoon."

"It is my pleasure, and it *will* brighten a dull afternoon for both of us. This I promise."

Recklessly, Indira accepted more vodka. "Fire away then, Commander, sir."

"Let's drop this rank stuff. If we are going to get anywhere at all, we have to begin by knowing and accepting each other. I'm scrap-heap material, too, Indira. I didn't have it anyway near as rough as you did. But, still, we're both on the junk heap. And that is what counts."

"Keep talking, Commander," she said. "I have nothing to lose."

He leaned forward. "But you have something to win."

"What would I possibly have to win?"

"A world for mankind. A planet called Kratos."

And then he told her what ExPEND was all about.

"There are twenty-five thousand million reasons why this project is needed—and they are all people, most of them living here on Terra. Sure we have colonies on Luna, Mars, Mercury, Venus and one or two of the satellites. But, all told, the solar colonists don't even account for one thousandth of one per cent of the total population." He gave a grim smile. "We have come too far too fast. This beat-up old planet is almost exhausted. Its fossil fuels are almost finished, and there are deserts where once good soil was over cropped. Earth can't take much more of the treatment mankind has been dishing out in the name of progress. What do we do with the people when population totally outstrips food production—as it surely will? We can't ship many to Mars because the planetary engineering programme will take centuries. And everywhere else you need total life-support systems . . . So, you either accept the proposition that mankind, being too bloody greedy, isn't worth saving. Or you have to try to create some way of ensuring that at least part of mankind survives —somewhere.

"About a hundred years ago, the futurologists saw the way it was all going. Eventually funds were provid-

ed by U.N. for two apparently impossible projects—
Faster Than Light drive and Matter Transmission.
They were crazy gambles that no responsible physicist
would want to touch. But man has a habit of pulling
off crazy gambles. So, while the Nobel prize-winners
looked the other way, the young men—the irrespon-
sible physicists, who asked why not, instead of why—
had their chance. Some of them blew themselves to
glory, simply demonstrating that two molecules can't be
in the same place at the same time."

"I am familiar with the history of F.T.L. and M.T.,"
interrupted Indira. "If the money spent on such projects had been used sensibly for reclamation here on
Terra, we might not be in such a jam now."

"Life on Terra was routed for disaster, anyway," retorted Conrad. "The point is, both projects have succeeded."

"I know. And the economics of both F.T.L. and
M.T. are frightening. It is cheaper to ship materials to
Mars, say, than to use matter transmission."

Conrad shrugged. "When the alternative is racial
suicide, high cost loses some of its importance."

"In any case," said Indira, "you can't transport people by either method. The trauma is too great. They go
crazy." She finished her vodka, wondering why she was
busy trying to talk herself out of a possible job. Probably an extension of the death wish.

Conrad showed signs of irritation. "Woman, do not
parade your ignorance! People have been experimentally transported by both methods."

"They came out sane?"

"They came out sane."

"How was it done?"

"Cold storage. Now, shut up and listen. Because the experiments were successful, mankind now has a real chance of survival. Not too great, maybe, but at least a chance. Hence the setting up of the Extra-Solar Planets Evaluating and Normalising Department. For the past twenty years small F.T.L. robot probes have been shot off in all directions at the nearer stars. They had to be robot probes because of the cost. When one of the probes finds a star with an Earth-type planet, it does an orbital survey then comes back with the data. Then, if the scientists think it is worth a try, we send people. Not colonists. Not until it has been proved that the planet can reasonably support human life. We send expendable people—people like you and me . . . Does it really matter to anyone whether you live or die, Indira Smith? I've checked the records, and I know it doesn't. Your parents are dead, you have no close surviving relatives, your boy-friend walked through a high window. I shall not be missed, either."

Indira was beginning to feel angry. It was true what he said about her—but it was the way he said it that hurt. It made her seem like a piece of human garbage. It offended her pride. She was amazed to discover that she had any pride left.

"And why will you not be missed, Commander?" she said silkily. "I understand you were something of a celebrity. I heard about your court-martial and, of course, I watched the resulting débâcle when you proved how tough you were. But a lot of people still seem to think you are some kind of hero. Why will you not be missed?"

He laughed grimly. "Like you, no surviving relatives

. . . It is true that the Space Service didn't actually fire me. I beat them to the draw . . . The plain fact is that I'm paranoid—at least, according to the psych boys. Therefore useless as far as the Space Service is concerned. The only authority I care to accept is my own. As commander of a team of Expendables, I will have absolute authority, which suits me fine. My qualifications are not, perhaps, as good as yours; but they are not bad . . . Now let us stop wasting time. I need a good second-in-command. The file and the results of your recent tests indicate that you are promising material. You would need some intensive training, of course . . . Yes or no?"

Indira was silent for a while. "I can't say that I like you very much, Commander Conrad," she began.

"So? It doesn't worry me. Also it is not too relevant. All I require is an honest answer, Lieutenant. Yes or no?"

"How big would the team be?"

"Seven human beings, six robots." Again he laughed. "Don't ask why the mystical number. It was arrived at by the think-tanks and the economists."

"What about the other five human beings? How do you intend to select them?"

"Like me and you, they will be totally expendable. They will probably be criminals and misfits—people who have nothing to lose. They will also have certain talents. I don't think there will be too much difficulty in recruitment. Well, Lieutenant Smith, let us not waste any more time. Yes or no?"

Indira took a deep breath. "Yes, damn you."

"Welcome aboard, then." He smiled. "In view of

your recent history, I suppose we shall have to train you to avoid being raped—especially since some of our enlisted men may have ambitions in that direction."

Indira said quietly: "Not necessary. If you don't believe me, try it yourself, Commander. These two legs of mine can kick your aspirations right out of your brain —or elsewhere—in nothing flat."

"I thought as much," he said calmly. "That is one of the reasons I chose you."

"The interview is over?" she asked.

"Yes, it's over. It wasn't too dreadful, was it?"

Indira stood up, swaying slightly. "You are a pretty inhuman bastard, Commander, sir."

Conrad shrugged. "That is the general opinion these days, apparently. Until you actually sign articles, Lieutenant, you can say what you like. After that you can only think what you like. Understood?"

"Understood."

Conrad also stood up. "I wonder if you would have dinner with me this evening? We might get to know each other better in less formal surroundings."

She gave a cynical smile. "Wine and dine, soft lights, the soft sell and a quick lay?"

Conrad gazed at her coldly. "That was not the intention. But since you imply it was, the invitation is cancelled."

"Thank you, Commander." She turned to go. "I'll try to bear my disappointment with fortitude."

"Thank you, Lieutenant," he retorted evenly. "Our professional relationship is what counts."

"I'll remember that."

When she had left, Conrad poured himself another drink—a large one—and sipped it meditatively. Lieu-

tenant Smith, he decided, was going to be a little difficult to handle. But that did not change his opinion that
she was right for the job.

EVENT THREE

Death in Orbit

Indira Smith had dined well, so had Conrad. Her first
meal, his second. Emerging from suspended animation
usually left people ravenously hungry for a day or
more. Like partial loss of memory, it was an after-
effect of the immense shock to which the body had
been subjected.

Indira's appetite was excellent, Conrad noted. She,
too, had made great inroads into the *Santa Maria's*
small and precious supplies of natural food. Later, everyone would have to live on concentrates, synthetic
foods and whatever edible things could be found on
Kratos. But, until the entire team of Expendables was
restored to full strength, its members would be entitled
to take in as much natural food as they wished.

After the meal, Conrad had taken Indira on a tour
of the vessel. She had never been—in a conscious condition—on a space ship before. And this was an F.T.L.
vessel. Its wonders confounded her. She had never seen
such sophisticated electronic equipment in her life.

The engine room—or reaction control complex, as it
was officially described—made her eyes widen with as-

tonishment. A master computer, no larger than a small desk, controlled three separate propulsion systems. The conventional rocket engines, used only for orbital manoeuvres, blast-off and touch-down; the thermo-nuclear drive, used for interplanetary travel; and the gravi-magnetic pulse generator that enabled the *Santa Maria* to create its own modified black hole in the space-time continuum to bridge the star gap at speed much faster than light. Conrad was able to explain the principle of rocket propulsion and thermo-nuclear drive easily. He had logged more space-hours than he cared to remember in vessels equipped with dual-system chemical and t/n propulsion. But he was still dazed by the gravi-magnetic pulse generator and cosmometer. The mathematicians and astrophysicists had patiently tried to explain their functions; but, somehow the message had not got across. It was still the white man's magic. And what the hell—the whole shebang was computer-controlled, any way. With F.T.L. a space captain, however good, was just supercargo. Chilled supercargo.

But he did try to tell Indira quite as much as he knew of the F.T.L. system.

"The point is," he said, "Einstein was both right and wrong. He was right in maintaining that no physical body could travel faster than light without achieving infinite mass. He was wrong that he did not forsee techniques that would allow the *Santa Maria* to opt out of conventional space-time mechanics. The pulse generator enables this vessel to create its own black hole in space and disappear like the proverbial Cheshire Cat. The cosmometer aligns its re-emergence in space-time with the desired destination." He sighed. "That's about all I know of F.T.L. and—so they told me—all I need to know. Well, the magic works . . . And here we are as the living proof . . . Sometimes, I wish I were back in the fifteenth century, when life was simple and a lot of people still believed the Earth was flat."

Impulsively, Indira held his hand. "We have come a long way from the flat Earth mentality," she said softly. "Let us hope it was all worth while."

Conrad laughed. "Amen to that. Let's go back to the nav deck and take a look at Kratos."

He kept her hand in his all the way. He rationalised by telling himself that she was not yet used to walking on bond-fuzz in zero gravity. You had to plant each foot very firmly on the carpet, so that the hooked bristles would grip the soles of your boots. Otherwise, you might take off and float helplessly.

Indira Smith, despite white hair and prosthetic legs (or was it because of them?) was a very attractive woman, compact and graceful. But, after the trauma of jumping sixteen light-years in S.A. the sex impulse was minimal. What mattered more was that she was a fellow human being, a companion with whom he would face as yet unknowable dangers, a vital member of the team that would either open up Kratos for mankind or, by perishing, prove that the planet was inimical to colonisation. That was why he held her hand. Because they both belonged to an elite company. The fraternity of the damned. The Expendables.

Besides, the physical contact generated warmth. In S.A. you were chilled and didn't feel it. Afterwards you were chilled because you had endured it. Not physically cold, but spiritually cold. Something that could only be combatted by the ancient magic of touch.

On the navigation deck, Conrad pressed the stud that rolled back the screen covering the observation panel. It was a good moment. The *Santa Maria* was just traversing from night-side to day-side. The planet of Kratos lay revealed in chiaroscuro.

There was no denying it was beautiful, but not so beautiful as Terra. Nor quite so complex. It had more ocean and only two major continental masses. The North Polar Continent was comparable in size, though not in shape, to Australia. It was, in fact, more like an elongated inverted South America with the narrow section straddling the pole and the bulge stretching well into the equatorial regions. The other land mass was similar in size and roughly similar in shape to Eurasia. The equator passed almost centrally through it; and it reached almost a third of the way round the planet. Apart from these great land masses, numerous archipelagos were revealed in the immense oceans.

As the *Santa Maria* moved slowly over day-side, Indira found the view breathtaking. "I had no idea it would look like this. It looks so tranquil, so utterly peaceful and lovely."

"So does Terra from a thousand miles up," said Conrad. He laughed. "Then you touch down and find it's not peaceful at all. Maybe that is the way it will be with Kratos."

"At least there won't be millions of competing and destructive human beings to foul it up," she retorted.

"No. Let's just hope we don't find millions of non-human beings who resent intruders."

"You think there will be intelligent animal life?"

He shrugged. "Look at it. An almost perfect evolutionary melting-pot—to mix metaphors. The surprising thing will be if we don't find any formidable animal life."

"I used the words intelligent, you used the word formidable."

"A man with an atomic weapon is both intelligent and formidable," explained Conrad patiently. "A black widow spider is not intelligent, but it is formidable. If the man with the atomic weapon doesn't like you and the spider doesn't like you, the end result can still be the same . . . I hope that there is nothing nasty in the woodshed, but I'm not betting on it."

"When do we go down?"

"When the entire team is in optimum condition. I have scheduled resuscitation of the rest at three hourly intervals. We will all need five T days, I think, to get our strength and our wits back."

"I think I am going to like working with you, Commander Conrad."

"I hope so. But drop this bloody rank stuff. I think I can still retain my authority even if in private you commit the dreadful indiscretion of calling me James."

She laughed. "Very well. I'm still hungry, James. I would sell my soul for a well-done steak."

"So am I, and you already have." He smiled. "Let's indulge ourselves. While the rest are coming out of the cooler, we will have an orgy of eating."

As he spoke one of the robots came to the nav deck. It was Luke.

"Emergency, sir. Mr. Kwango fails to respond to resuscitation procedure. All available techniques have been applied."

"Then apply them again," snapped Conrad. "I'm

damned if I'm going to touch down with one of my team already dead."

"No, wait!" There was suddenly a note of command in Indira's voice. "What is the oesophagal temperature Luke?"

"Thirty-six point nine degrees, Lieutenant."

"Get it down fifteen degrees as quickly as you can. Hurry."

Somehow, Luke contrived to look pained. "Temperature reduction is already commencing, Lieutenant."

"I'm sorry." Indira had forgotten that the robots were radio linked.

"Query, Lieutenant. Why are you sorry? Decision is being executed."

"Cancel statement," said Conrad, more familiar with the ways of the robotic mind. He turned to Indira. "What are you going to do?"

"First, I am going to examine my patient," she said. "Then I shall either decide upon a second attempt at resuscitation or perform a heart transplant . . . Luke, get the theatre ready in case we need it."

"Decision noted. Execution in progress."

"You are in no shape to make a heart transplant," exploded Conrad. "You are only just out of S.A. yourself. You are still shaky and weak."

"It is my duty to do the best I can for my patient," she retorted coolly.

"And it is my duty," said Conrad, "to do the best I can for my entire team. You are weak, you lack energy, you need food and rest. Until I am convinced that you are in optimum condition, you will not even look at Kwango. That is an order."

"Very well, Commander." Her voice was hard. She

spoke once more to Luke. "Continue temperature reduction to standard S.A. level."

"Decision noted, Lieutenant."

"And then stick him back in the cooler," added Conrad. "After which, proceed with resuscitation of Mr. Andreas."

"Decision noted, sir."

"Then execute!" grated Conrad unnecessarily. He turned to Indira. "You are going to eat a well-done steak—or whatever else you want—and drink a couple of glasses of wine. Then you are going to rest for at least six hours. After that, we'll review the situation."

"I am no longer hungry." Her voice was angry. "It is my professional opinion, Commander Conrad, that I should attend to my patient now."

"And it is my professional opinion, Lieutenant Smith, that you should eat and rest. I will enter your protest in the log. But you will obey my order."

"Yes, sir!" she saluted insolently.

Conrad sighed. It was going to be a long time before he held Indira Smith's hand again. Not that it mattered . . .

FLASH THREE

The Team

Conrad looked at the faces he had come to know so well—the six other people who would form his team of Expendables. This was the first time he had brought them all together. He had given them their preliminary briefings individually. Now, sitting on the mats in this gymnasium, and wearing light track suits, they were assembled. Would they make a successful team? He had to find out fast.

"Ladies and gentlemen, I know all of you intimately. But you do not know each other. We will rectify that. Because if we are to work as a team, there can be no secrets among us. First, I will declare myself. I am a disgraced space-captain—or was. I was court-martialled for refusing to obey orders and thereby endangering lives. Several people died because I made a wrong decision. I drink too much and tend to be violent, but never when on duty. The psychiatrists claim that I have a paranoid mind. This is all I have to say about myself. The rest you will discover later. Now let us begin the process of introduction. As I call your name, please stand up. Lou Andreas."

The big man lifted himself to his feet. He looked at the rest and grinned good-naturedly.

"Lou Andreas is an American," said Conrad. "He is kind and considerate, and he likes children. Unfortunately, he managed to kill a fair number in a freeway accident by driving his turbocar dangerously because he'd quarrelled with his girl-friend. Lou is a first class engineer, but a little temperamental. Let's hope he gets less temperamental because some day our lives may depend on him. Thank you, Lou."

The big man shrugged and sat down again.

"Fidel Batista."

A slender, nervous-looking man stood up.

"Fidel Batista is Cuban. He was a professional political assassin and was sentenced to life imprisonment in Algeria for the assassination of President Gallienne. He is a good man to have for you, and a bad one to have against you. He is a weapons and explosives expert. Thank you, Fidel."

Batista flashed an insolent glance at Conrad and sat down.

"Elizabeth James."

A well-built, attractive but not beautiful woman stood up. She had short dark hair and a rounded face.

"Liz James is British."

"Welsh, Commander."

Conrad smiled. "All right, Welsh. Like Fidel, she has a weakness for violent politics. Like Guy Fawkes, she tried to put the British parliament in orbit. Like Guy Fawkes, she failed. Perhaps because basically she is a biologist. Thank you, Liz."

"Thank you, Commander." Despite the track suit, Liz managed to sit down as if she were inviting someone to seduce her.

"Chantana Le Gros."

A dark, petite and very beautiful woman stood up.

"Chantana Le Gros is Vietnamese-French. She looks fragile, but isn't. She was married twice, and poisoned both husbands—for personal reasons. She was under sentence of death when recruited. She is a chemist of distinction."

Chantana rewarded Conrad with a faint smile and resumed her position on the mat gracefully, appearing to withdraw into contemplation.

"Kurt Kwango."

A black man of imposing stature stood up. He flexed his muscles as if anticipating combat.

"Kurt Kwango is Nigerian, but his mother was German. As you see, the negro genes are dominant. Kurt has a long history of violence including attempted murder, grievous bodily harm and rape. He is also an outstanding ecologist. Try to be nice to him. We may need his talents."

Kurt Kwango laughed. "Thank you, suh, Massa Boss."

Conrad said evenly: "Sit down, Kurt. You are overplaying it."

Kurt grinned. "Allus willin' to oblige de white master." He sat.

"Kurt also has a dreadful sense of humour," added Conrad. "It may keep us horrified during the tedium of trying to tame an unknown planet . . . And now our final guest appearance. Surgeon Lieutenant Indira

Smith, late of the Terran Disaster Corps. Stand, Lieutenant Smith and let them see you."

Indira stood.

"Unlike the rest of us," went on Conrad, "she has committed no crime against society. Her luck ran out with a bunch of so-called freedom fighters in Brazil. They liberated her body then cut off her legs. But, as you can see, she has new legs. She is my second-in-command. She is a good surgeon. Let us hope none of us will need her services."

A hand shot up. Kurt Kwango spoke. "What fo' you take a woman second-in-command, Massa Boss? Is you all plumb crazy or does you shack up wid de pretty little gel?"

"Stand, Kwango!" Conrad's voice seemed to have a cutting edge. "And cut the Uncle Tom stuff. We need you. But you are not irreplaceable."

Kurt Kwango stood. "Yes, suh," he mocked. "Ah understands you good and plenty."

"You fancy Lieutenant Smith—even though she has artificial legs?"

"Yes, suh," grinned Kurt. "De tin legs don't worry me none."

"Then take her, black man. She's all yours. Who knows, *you* may be good enough to be my Number One."

The rest of the team moved back and left the mats free. Indira stood still, slightly crouching, facing Kurt. He made some feinting moves. She did not respond.

Lou Andreas jeered. "You're not so hot, Kwango. You get your bangs in the geriatrics ward?"

Kurt growled angrily, and lunged forward, his arms outstretched, hoping to throw Indira to the mat. She waited almost until he was about to connect. Then, suddenly, she wasn't there. Her legs seemed to straighten like pieces of spring steel as she leaped nearly three metres into the air.

Kurt stared up in amazement. It was a mistake. As Indira came down, she expertly tapped him on the chin with her foot. He fell backwards like a log, and lay on the mat twitching. Indira landed perfectly.

Conrad glanced at Kurt Kwango with a faint smile. "I hope you didn't hurt him too much, Lieutenant Smith."

"No," said Indira quietly. "It would have been easy to separate his head from his body, but I didn't hurt him . . . I hope he *is* a good ecologist."

"Good, but wayward. Incidentally, his I.Q. is more than twenty points higher than yours or mine."

Kurt sat up, rubbed his jaw and looked rather foolish.

Conrad surveyed the rest of the team. "Now you know one of the reasons why Lieutenant Smith is second-in-command. We all have a lot to learn about each other. Most important of all, we have to learn to trust and respect each other. We have two weeks to prove ourselves. This afternoon will be devoted to unarmed combat. Clear the mats."

EVENT FOUR

The Resurrection and the Life

Conrad had been looking for Indira all over the ship. She had not responded to intercom calls, and she was not in her cabin. The last place he thought of looking for her was the library. That is where he found her, running micro-film through the viewer.

"Why didn't you answer my calls? You must have heard them."

"I heard them," she said coldly. "I was busy."

"Four hours ago I ordered you to relax for at least six hours."

"I know." She gave him a thin smile. "I found it difficult to relax by order, Commander. What now? Are you going to have me drummed out of the service for insubordination? We are a long way from home."

Conrad managed to suppress his anger. He noted the signs of fatigue on her face. She was a woman who was driving herself hard. It would not help now if he added to her problems. But later, he promised himself, when the present crisis was resolved—one way or another—Indira Smith would get a taste of discipline.

"Let's stop fighting," he said gently, "and go back to square one. What have you been doing?"

She looked up from the viewer and faced him. 'I did try to rest. But you can't command a surgeon to relax when someone's life is at stake."

"So?"

"So I took a blood sample and analysed it. Some careless bastard back on Earth failed to give Kurt Kwango his sub-thermal shock injection."

"What the hell does that mean?"

"Do you know anything about vintage cars, Commander?"

The question took him by surprise. "I have had the privilege of driving a 1980 Rolls Royce in the London to Brighton race."

"Petroleum-powered?"

"Of course. Hydrocarbon fuels were still available when it was built."

"Then, if I am not mistaken, it had a water-cooling system."

"Yes. What has this to do with Kwango?"

"Bear with me. In winter, how would you protect the cooling system?"

"Simple. I'd mix anti-freeze solution with the water."

"And if you failed to do so, and there was a heavy frost?"

"Ice could form and eventually crack the cylinder block . . ." Suddenly, Conrad saw what she was getting at.

"Unlike your Rolls Royce, we human beings don't have cooling systems, we have heating systems. The blood we pump round is mostly composed of water. The sub-thermal shock injection has several functions; but, like your anti-freeze solution, it also lowers the temperature at which ice crystals will form. And, if you don't use it, the consequences can be roughly the same . . . Kwango's heart is ruined." She gave a bitter laugh. "Wonderful, isn't it? We can travel faster than light to Altair, but some cretinous medic sixteen light-years away puts the venture at risk because he forgot to give a sample shot."

"Maybe Kurt ducked it," suggested Conrad.

"Why should he do that?"

Conrad shrugged. "How the hell should I know? It's possible, that's all. Kurt is a very temperamental character, as we have discovered. Maybe he doesn't like needles being pushed into him . . . There are so many fail-safe procedures in space-flight preparation that I find it hard to believe a man's life could depend on one medic's absent-mindedness, or whatever."

"Well, it happened. To us, the reason why it happened can only be of academic interest."

Conrad asked a stupid question. "Can anything be done?"

"Of course," she snapped. "I'm the bloody surgeon of this crazy outfit. Among my stores there are three electro-mechanical hearts powered by micropiles, and three bio-hearts. If you will leave me alone, I'll try to decide which is best for Kurt Kwango . . . Dammit, I'm not a heart surgeon and I have a lot of learning to do."

"I'm sorry, Lieutenant Smith." Conrad accepted his dismissal and turned to go. "You have had a rough awakening."

"Wait . . . I'm sorry, too, Commander. I'll do my

best. That's all I can promise . . . How—how are things going?"

"Lou Andreas and Liz James are now safely out of S.A. They ate well, and they are resting."

"Good. So that only leaves Chantana and Fidel. Can they wait?"

Conrad smiled faintly. "I don't think they will protest."

"Then I would like the theatre prepared for a transplant . . . It was Matthew, wasn't it, who was given the extended med-programming?"

"Yes, it was."

"Then he will know what to do. Tell him it's a low-temperature job. I shall probably use thermal lances. I want the body and the environment at about two degrees Centigrade. But I also want infra-red and environmental heat available on command. And I want the heart-lung machine and the coronary pump readied. I will operate two hours from now."

"How many robots do you want attending?"

"Matthew is the only one trained for theatre work."

"That doesn't matter," said Conrad patiently. "He has control circuits."

"Yes." She brushed a hand over her head. "I forgot. I'll have two besides Matthew."

"Would you like me to be present?"

She threw back the question. "Do you want to be present?"

"Yes. I'm not good for much but moral support, but I'd like to be there."

"If you pass out, Commander, you'll only be a nuisance. But if you vomit, you'll very likely release enough bugs to kill Kwango."

"I have a strong stomach, and I have dealt with badly wounded men."

"This is different. I shall systematically open the chest and cut out the heart of someone you know."

"If it won't inconvenience you, I would still like to be there."

She gave him a thin smile. "It won't inconvenience me. Now let me get on with my work, Commander. Matthew will instruct you in pre-op sterilising procedure."

"One question. Have you ever done this before?"

"No, Commander. But then we Expendables have already stacked up quite a number of firsts, haven't we?"

Lieutenant Smith had finally decided to use a bio-heart. It had been donated by some unfortunate man who died in a hovercar pile-up sixteen light-years away. It was now resting in a fluid cradle, hooked up to a coronary pump. Oxygenated blood pulsed through the heart, causing it to beat with the illusion of independent life.

On the operating table lay Kurt Kwango, his magnificent body curiously shrunken. Surgeon Lieutenant Smith had already opened his chest with a straight cut down the centre, cauterising the blood vessels. Now she took an electric saw and split the breast-bone. Steam rose from the open wound. Deftly Matthew inserted a retractor, drawing apart the rib cage.

Conrad watched grimly. Lieutenant Smith did not need to give many instructions. It was as if Matthew had an intuitive knowledge of her needs.

The pericardial sac was exposed.

Matthew handed Lieutenant Smith a pair of scissors. She opened the thin sac. Kwango's heart was revealed.

"Make ready for by-pass." Indira's voice was abnormally calm. The robot Mark instantly began to prepare the linkage with the heart-lung machine.

Because the operation was being conducted in zero G, tiny globules of blood rose from the body and were immediately sucked up by the vacuum cleaner whose metallic mouth hovered over the operating table.

Conrad, himself gowned and masked in irradiated and sterile fabric watched, fascinated, as Lieutenant Smith deftly continued her work of preparing for the by-pass. Presently, the arterial and venous tubes were connected. The time had come for Kurt Kwango's dead heart to be removed from his body.

"By-pass ready, Matthew?"

"Yes, Lieutenant. By-pass ready." Matthew's gowned figure looked oddly human.

Indira Smith straightened her back and met Conrad's gaze. "Now we go for the big one." She lifted a scalpel, and glanced briefly at Matthew. "Start the pump."

Electric motors began to whirr. Blood pulsed through plastic tubing and was pumped rhythmically into Kwango's cardio-vascular system. The oxygenated blood that, hopefully, would bring a dead man back to life.

Until the dead heart had been removed and the donor heart fully implanted, the heart-lung machine was all that kept Kwango's temporary death from being permanent.

Conrad watched, fascinated. He did not know how

long he watched. Time had become irrelevant. He was aware not of the passing of time, only of the occurrence of significant events.

He saw Indira Smith lift the dead heart out of Kwango's chest and place it almost reverently into a white pan.

Later—was it minutes or hours? He did not know— he saw her disconnect the donor heart from its support system and place it in the cavity in Kwango's chest. Then, after the suckers had drained the pericardium of blood, she began to sew up the aortic connections with ferocious intensity.

Conrad watched, not understanding, but knowing that he was witnessing an heroic struggle.

"Cut the pump!" snapped Indira. A robot—which was it?—instantly complied.

"Run up the heat programme. I want an even thirty-six degrees fast!"

The donor heart began to fibrillate.

"Defibrillation—quickly!"

A robot handed Indira two metal discs with wires attached to them that led to a small metal box.

Indira placed them on each side of the donor heart.

As Kurt Kwango received the electric shock, his body arched with a fantastic and instantaneous illusion of independent life. Then suddenly the donor heart began to beat.

Surgeon-Lieutenant Smith uttered a great sigh. She looked at Matthew. "Pressure and pulse, please."

"Pressure 85, pulse 110."

"Temperature?"

"34-4."

Surgeon-Lieutenant Smith looked at Conrad once more. "I think we have made it, Commander. All that remains are the mopping up operations." She glanced at the tiny globules of blood still being sucked up by the vacuum cleaner. "And, of course, I have to close the chest."

"Lieutenant," said Conrad, trying to keep his voice calm. "If we survive, I shall recommend you for D.S.S.C."

"Recommend a cup of coffee," said Indira Smith. "By God, I need it!"

Later, on the navigation deck, as they sipped coffee and gazed at the enigmatic face of Kratos once more, Conrad said: "You and I have to stop fighting. Otherwise, we put this whole bloody project at risk."

"Were we fighting?" she asked drily. "I hadn't noticed it."

"Don't be stupid. You know damn well what I mean."

She appeared to ignore his remark. "There is the planet that will make us or break us, Commander. It looks so tranquil, so beautiful, it is hard to think it could be dangerous."

"It will neither make us or break us," he snapped. "We shall prove it, or it will kill us. And if we are going to prove it, there must be no serious dissension between you and me. Get it into your head that personal feelings don't matter very much. The only thing that matters is that we try as hard as we can to prove Kratos suitable for colonisation. And that will need discipline. Message ends."

Indira Smith gave a great sigh, or a yawn. "I'm sorry if I have been a bit of a cow, Commander. But Kwango lives, does he not?"

"Yes, thanks to you, Kwango lives."

"Good." And then she fainted. Her body floated gracefully in zero G. She still held the half-empty plastic bulb of coffee limply in her hand. Conrad looked at the lines of fatigue on her face, the dark circles round her eyes. Then, expertly, he took hold of her and cradled her like a child.

FLASH FOUR

Proving Ground

Conrad was proud. They had made the summit of the Matterhorn by the North face. Not a bad achievement. Seven men and women, none of them trained climbers, had taken a crash course, roped themselves together, and placed their trust in each other. The gamble had paid off. So here they were at the summit, with numbed faces and half-frozen limbs, waiting for the chopper to lift them out.

Conrad surveyed his team. There had been a bad moment when Chantana Le Gros lost her footing and swung out into space with a thousand metre drop below her. But Kurt Kwango—fourth in line and directly above her—had kept his head, using his magnificent strength to haul her to safety.

"At least we are alive," said Conrad painfully, as ice formed on his lips. "That's not bad for amateurs. Kurt you did a great job."

Kurt Kwango as shivering and almost exhausted, but he managed to laugh. "Thank you, Massa Boss. I was already calculating her impact velocity. Then I decided she was too pretty to die."

Conrad could hear the sound of the chopper coming from behind him. "Next we go fry outselves in an open boat in the Pacific," he said. "After that, we'll try a rest cure in the Malayan jungle. And after that—if we still survive as a team, we'll familiarise ourselves with some of the hardware we'll have to use on Kratos."

"Commander, this here course looks as if it is going to be a real fun thing," drawled Lou Andreas. "Don't we get no leave?"

"What the hell would you do with leave?" demanded Conrad. "You are an Expendable, Lou. You'll get leave—if you are still alive and if you still want it—when we have proved Kratos. Now make ready for lift-off in the following order . . ."

The chopper came as low as it could.

Three days without food or fresh water in a standard fibre-glass lifeboat in the middle of the Pacific ocean had revealed many tensions in the team. Fidel Batista, suffering from heat stroke and frequently taunted by Lou Andreas, had tried to kill him with a knife. Conrad had taken the knife blow on his prosthetic arm. On the second day, out of sheer boredom, Liz James had offered herself to any man with the strength left to take her. Kwango had tried; but dehydration was too much for him. Temperamental as ever he jumped overboard in sheer self-disgust. Maybe he just wanted to cool off.

But the sharks seemed to have anticipated the precise moment. Andreas, Batista and Le Gros went after him—with knives, the only weapons in the boat. Batista had a piece bitten out of his left buttock. But they all managed to get back aboard with Kwango.

It was a near thing. Conrad was very glad when the chopper appeared and took them out.

Batista was lucky. While the rest of them were on a six-day crash course in jungle survival, he was having his buttock repaired.

Chantana Le Gros was very good in the jungle. So was Kurt Kwango. Lou Andreas and Liz James were not. Lou seemed to act as a magnet for wild life, from leeches to snakes. Liz was a casualty to the high temperature and humidity. This time there was no chopper to search them out. They had to make their way through a hundred kilometres of very dense jungle to a pre-arranged take-out point. Twice, Lieutenant Smith had to take snake venom out of Lou. Liz managed to last four days before she succumbed to heat stroke. They made a litter for her. She tried not to use it too much, knowing that most of the others were near to exhaustion. To her credit, she insisted on walking the last fourteen kilometres. Then she went out like a light.

Conrad wiped his face, swollen and disfigured by insect bites, running with sweat. As the medics lifted Liz on to a stretcher, he said: "I guess we are learning as much about ourselves as about each other. How much longer could you have taken it, Kurt?"

The Nigerian smiled. "Longer than you, Commander." But there was no insolence in his voice.

Conrad grinned. "I guess you could. So could Chantana. How about you, Indira?"

"I had an advantage. My legs never got tired."

"Now let's go where they serve ice-cold gin and tonics in a civilised fashion. We have proved ourselves to be a team; and the worst that has happened is that Fidel can't sit down."

"He helped save my stupid life," said Kurt. "I will remember that."

"Wrong," said Conrad lightly. "He saved a stupid ecologist."

"You saved my life also, Kurt," said Chantana, "on that dreadful mountain. I, too, will not forget."

Kwango laughed. "I save the woman, not the biologist," he retorted. "Enlightened self-interest. One has to think of the future."

"Yes," said Conrad, "the time has come to think carefully of the future. Tomorrow, while we blast to Kennedy, I'll tell you about Kratos."

EVENT FIVE

Touch Down

The rocket engines died. There was silence. Everyone except Kurt Kwango, who was confined to the sterile chamber, was lying securely strapped in contour-berths on the navigation deck. The robots, virtually unaffected by the G-stress of touch-down deceleration, were carrying out their appointed tasks. Matthew was in the sterile chamber with Kwango, monitoring his heart reaction, temperature and breathing cycle, and relaying this data to Indira Smith. Mark was in the theatre, readying it for anyone who succumbed to G-stress. Luke and John were in the engine-room, available to manually override the computer-controlled touch-down if the Commander should require it. Peter and Paul were already in the air-lock, assembling their equipment for a preliminary survey of the immediate touch-down area.

Conrad unfastened his belts and got out of his contour-birth. Being a trained spaceman, he was the first to recover from G-stress. The touch-down had been perfect. No problems. He was slightly annoyed that the computer had managed it so well.

"Ladies and gentlemen, that's it. We have arrived. I suppose it is—or could be, if our mission is successful —an historic moment. Maybe I ought to make a speech, but I don't feel like it. There is a lot to be done before any of us gets outside the air-lock. First of all, get out of your berths, stand up, try walking."

Chantana Le Gros's legs gave way. She fell on to the deck, a comical look of amazement on her face.

"Problem one," said Conrad. "Our muscles have been weakened by S.A. and twenty-three E-days in zero G. I would have liked to touch down much earlier, but Lieutenant Smith advised against it. Kwango's acceptance of his new heart was good, but obviously he could not take the G-factor necessary for deceleration soon after a heart transplant . . . What is the latest information from the sterile chamber, Lieutenant?"

"My patient is still unconscious, but his responses are good. He should regain consciousness. The shot I gave him would knock him out for not more than two hours."

"That is all right, then. Kwango will not return to active service until Lieutenant Smith says so. But the rest of you are under starter's orders, and I am the starter. One, for the first three K-days, no one will venture outside the *Santa Maria*. Two, all of us will take one-hour work-outs in the gym at six-hour intervals. Three, the robots will shortly make surveys of our immediate vicinity, collecting samples and specimens. Four, those of you with the appropriate skills will study or analyse such objects and present me with preliminary findings as soon as possible. Five, while we are in this phase of intensive make-ready, you will be allowed to eat what you wish when you wish. Afterwards, a ration system will be introduced. Six, no alcohol will be consumed without permission from me. Do you all read me?"

"We read you loud and clear, Commander." It was Lou Andreas who spoke. "All work and no play. We get the message."

Conrad glanced briefly at Liz James. "Definitely no play. Not yet. We are here to do a job, and, by God, we'll do it. Which leads me to one other point, which must be dealt with before any of us goes outside. Casualties. There are only seven of us, so we cannot afford to be reckless. No one will put himself or herself at risk without clearance. We cannot afford death or incapacitation by carelessness. However, accidents may happen. We must be prepared for them. In the event of my death or incapacitation, Lieutenant Smith will assume command. In the event of her death or incapacitation, Mr. Andreas will assume command. In the event of his death, Miss Le Gros will assume command, with the instruction—which I will record in the log—to pull out. O.K.?"

There was a moment or two of silence. Then Chantana Le Gros spoke. "This is fine, in theory, Commander. But I do not know how to handle a space-ship."

"Matthew does," retorted Conrad. "He and his happy band are entirely familiar with recall procedure. Also they are familiar with S.A. techniques. Give the commands, Chantana, and they will be carried out. Next thing you know, you'll take up in Earth orbit. Let's hope it won't come to that."

Fidel Batista crossed himself. "Let us hope, indeed."

"Well, then," said Conrad. "Let's take a look at this

world we have come sixteen light years to make fit for human habitation."

He pressed a stud on the command console. A screen rolled back to reveal the observation panel. Because the *Santa Maria* was ninety metres high, it was impossible to look straight down. But the panel showed a stretch of what looked to be flat grassland, then forest and, in the distance, a range of hills. In the middle distance a network of the mysterious ruts of Kratos was visible.

"It's a fine morning," said Liz James with a note of incredulity in her voice, as she glanced up at the blue, cloud-flecked sky. "You could almost believe that you were back on Earth. Apart from the ruts."

"Apart from the ruts," echoed Conrad. "I chose this area, which is semi-tropical, because those damned ruts have their densest configurations in the tropical and semi-tropical zones—particularly on this land mass, Continent B."

A robot's voice came over the intercom. "Peter reporting, Commander. Survey equipment ready and checked."

"These are my instructions," said Conrad. "You will proceed through air-lock, release nylon ladder and transfer equipment dirtside. You will then inspect landing torus for possible damage and report back. You will also determine attitude of this vessel and report back. If no damage, and if attitude lies within acceptable parameter, you will proceed as follows: one, you will set up the four vid cameras and test hook-in to command screens; two, you will collect samples as already specified; three, you will sweep an area of one thousand metres radius from the *Santa Maria*. If any hostile life-form is encountered, you will return without accepting any risk. Execute."

"Decisions noted, Commander. Execution proceeding."

Damage to the large landing torus with its flexible base was minimal. Some of the titanium cladding had been dented on impact, but it as no more than was expected. The attitude of the vessel was four point five degrees from the vertical, but this also was acceptable.

No problems there. Conrad was relieved. At touchdown the first duty of a master was to verify the safety of his vessel. Within half an hour the robot had set up the vid cameras, each on a tripod with a variable-speed rotating mechanism on the support head. Conrad ordered two of the cameras to be set on one-minute revolution and two on three-minute revolutions. Thus the immediate vicinity of the *Santa Maria* would be constantly under surveillance. The pictures were relayed to a bank of four screens on the nav deck.

So now, while the robots set about their task of collecting samples, it would be possible to study the environs of the ship in detail.

The six Expendables gazed at the vid screens in fascination—perhaps prepared for anything other than the utter normality which soon became apparent. They had touched down on a planet sixteen light years from Earth. They would have been less surprised if the ground had opened to spew forth monsters than they were at the eerie familiarity of the scenes displayed. The grassland, in the midst of which the *Santa Maria* sat, looked almost exactly like terrestrial grassland in high summer. There were several birds, obviously not identifiable, but demonstrably birds, lazily circling or

gliding in the sky; and there was a number of butterflies flitting neurotically round some small shrubs about
fifty metres from touch-down. It was all so abnormally
normal. It produced a feeling of anti-climax.

Conrad sensed the sudden surge of confidence.
"Don't be fooled by the rural setting," he warned.
"Those birds, for all we know, could be lethal to
human beings. Those butterflies could be carnivorous
or carry a nasty sting in their tails. Until we have col-
lected and analysed samples, we must assume the
worst."

After the robots had delivered samples of air, vegetation and soil to the vessel's air-lock, they began their
thousand-metre sweep, moving out from the *Santa
Maria* in a spiral path. The birds treated them with
total indifference. The butterflies fluttered away at their
approach. Two small creatures, observable only by
their furry backs as they bounded away from the advancing robots, were the only signs of animal life revealed.

"They look like hares," said Liz James.

"More like baby kangaroos," amended Chantana Le
Gros. "One had a long spatulate tail that seemed to be
used for balance and thrust. Did anyone else see it?"

No one had.

Conrad said: "So far so good, but—I repeat—do
not be lulled into complacency by this other Eden . . .
Now, we all have work to do. James and Le Gros,
please collect the samples from the air-lock and give
me your findings as soon as possible. Andreas and Batista will continue to minitor the screens. I will hit the
paper work. Lieutenant Smith, when you have checked

your patient, perhaps you will give any assistance that may be required to James and Le Gros."

"Yes, Commander."

It was at that point that one of the robots disappeared.

FLASH FIVE

Briefing

The Trans-Terra strato-rocket was fifteen miles up, high enough for the stars to be seen in day-time through a permanent violet twilight. The rocket would cover the ten thousand miles from Singapore to Mexico City in less than two hours. From Mexico City a local sub-strato jet would lift the Expendables across the Gulf of Mexico, over the Florida peninsula to Kennedy Space Port.

With the exception of Conrad, this was the nearest that the team had ever been to the space frontier. Most of them gazed through the observation panels. Even Kurt Kwango, who was working out a nasty 3D chess problem involving knight and queen moves near the centre of the cube, cast an occasional glance at the awesome splendour of the starry deeps.

Conrad thought the time had come.

"Out there," he said gesturing to one of the observation panels, "is a star called Altair. It's sixteen light years away—practically next door, astronomically speaking. A robot probe says it has five planets. The probe inspected all of them in low-level orbit. Finally it concentrated on Altair Four. Altair Four has been designated Earth-type. That is to say, it has an oxygen-nitrogen atmosphere, its surface temperatures fall within Terran extremes, it has three times as much sea area as land area, and its G-force is one point fifteen, which shouldn't worry us too much. Most of the land area, except for polar regions, is rich with vegetation. Animal life was detected, but there were no signs of technologically advanced civilisation.

"It is a tradition among Terran astronomers to assign a classical name, mythological or historical, to new discoveries. So Altair Four has been given the name of Kratos. In mythology, Kratos is the son of Nike, Greek goddess of victory. The word Kratos means strength. Let us assume, then, some clairvoyance on the part of our chairborne friends. Let us assume that Kratos is going to be tough. If so, our task is to lick it into shape, to prove that colonists can survive there and flourish. Some of us may die there—which doesn't matter too much, since we are all socially expendable. But, as a team, we have to prove the planet one way or the other. We have to prove that it's O.K. for colonists or that it is certain death."

"Suppose Kratos has people?" said Kurt Kwango, emerging from the fascinating problems of a centre cube knight move. "What do we do—hoist the U.N. flag and tell them that we have come to liberate them?" He gazed at Conrad quizzically.

"A good question, Kurt. How do you define people?"

"As animals capable of conceptual thought, social organisation and the use of tools."

"Well, if we find any such animals, we will have to

refer back to Terra. If they are an intelligent race, we will not be allowed to exploit them or modify their environment or interfere with their social structure."

Kurt laughed. "Commander, when the slavers came to Africa, a lot of people voiced the same fine sentiments. But the slavers won."

"They lost in the end, Kurt. Because of that, we have learned something."

"I hope so, Commander Conrad, I truly hope so."

"There is one disturbing fact about Kratos," went on Conrad. "The planetary surface, particularly in the tropical regions, is marred by deep ruts. They present a strange pattern, looking almost like pathways gouged out of the ground. The robot probes were unable to obtain data that would explain this phenomenon. Our priority assignment is to discover how and why the ruts were made."

"What do the people think who analysed the probe data?" It was Fidel Batista asking. Apart from Conrad, Batista was the only one standing in the rocket's tiny conference room. He was standing because he could not yet comfortably sit . . .

Conrad smiled. "As usual the scientists are divided. Some of the wild ones are thinking in terms of an abandoned and elaborate system of irrigation or transport canals. Some of the less wild ones suggest continuous minor planet quakes. Others have dreamed up volcanic eruption, some form of natural radio-active leakage, and even animal migration routes."

"What's your best, Commander?" asked Liz James.

"I place no bets. We are going to find out."

The flat voice of the robotpilot came over the intercom:

"Minus twenty minutes to touch-down, ladies and gentlemen. Please go to your contour-berths and prepare to accept one point five G for eleven minutes, two point two five G thereafter. Weather in Mexico City is fine, hot and humid."

Fidel Batista winced. Two point two five G was going to be excrutiating.

EVENT SIX

Base One

The robot that disappeared was Paul. In the four seconds before his destruction—being programmed only to obtain and transmit data, and not being programmed to experience fear—he relayed what information he could.

"I am falling down a circular shaft which was concealed by a thin surface layer. The shaft appears to be machine—"

Transmission ended. Presumably Paul had hit the bottom and was destroyed on impact.

All transmissions from the two robots assigned to preliminary investigations were taped. Conrad had timed the playback. Knowing the G-force of Kratos, it was possible to assign a fall rate of ten metres per second. Therefore Conrad was able to calculate that the shaft was about one hundred metres deep.

While the rest of the team continued their assigned tasks, he went out to investigate. Although the atmosphere of Kratos was acceptable to human beings, he took no chances, not yet having had the lab report on micro-organisms. He wore an armoured space suit and took with him the robot Luke, who carried one hundred and fifty metres of nylon rope.

The hole was seven hundred metres from the *Santa Maria.* Peter stood close by it. Before Conrad and Luke arrived, Peter had already discovered another circular patch of apparently firm ground on which no grass grew. Upon his own initiative, he had found and thrown a ten-kilo rock on to the bare patch. The crust had disintegrated, revealing yet another circular shaft.

Conrad inspected both. Then he came back to the hole down which Paul had fallen.

He tied the rope round the waist of his space suit. "I'm going down. Peter, Luke, you will both hold the rope, standing two metres from the brink. You will pay out the rope so that I descend at the rate of one metre per second. Execute."

Luke said: "Commander, would it not be more efficient to send one of us down the shaft?"

Conrad realised with some amusement that the robot was being subtle. What he would have said—if his inhibiting circuits had allowed it—would have been something like: "Commander, don't be a bloody fool. Don't hazard a human being, send a machine."

"I want to see for myself," said Conrad. "Execute."

He saw for himself. The robots lowered him at precisely one metre per second down one hundred and ten metres of vertical and perfectly cylindrical shaft.

Conrad had his headlamp on. He noted that the wall of the shaft seemed fused, almost glassy—as if it had been subjected to intense heat or, possibly, some powerful chemical. One hundred and ten metres down, he found the wreckage of Paul. One glance told him that the robot could not be salvaged. Leading off from the shaft was a horizontal tunnel, also circular, also two metres in diameter. He did not investigate further. He signalled to be hauled up.

Back aboard the *Santa Maria,* he received the lab reports on samples of soil, vegetation and air. The most important information was that there were no organisms inimical to human beings.

"O.K. then," he said. "We can establish a surface base. The robots will erect a perimeter defence/alarm system at a radius of one hundred metres from the ship. Within this area, we have established that there are none of the concealed shafts which took the starch out of Paul."

"Commander," said Lou Andreas, "you've been outside and survived. I feel in pretty good shape right now. Maybe I could help the robots to—"

"Not a chance, Mr. Andreas," cut in Conrad firmly. "Your services are required on board. There is a lot of hardware to be tested and made ready. I'll get the manifest and give you a list of priorities. Lieutenant Smith still has to look after Kwango and, when she has the time, assist James and Le Gros in the lab. That leaves Batista to continue monitoring the screens. I shall be pretty busy myself. But when any of us have free time we will give Batista a break from getting square eyes. O.K. Fidel?"

"O.K. Commander."

"I anticipate that we will do our eating and sleeping in the ship for several days," went on Conrad. "But after the mandatory three days aboard—by which time Base One should be reasonably proved as a safe area— we will all take acclimatisation spells."

"Aren't you being unnecessarily cautious?" enquired Liz James. "The air samples are O.K. The immediate flora and fauna present no problems."

"James, at all times you will address me as Commander or sir," snapped Conrad irritably.

"Yes, Commander, sir." She stood up and thrust out her breasts with studied insolence.

"As to your question, I am not being unnecessarily cautious. I have just lost one robot. I cannot afford to lose people. You have your assignments. Go see to them. I want detailed analysis of the bio-function of every specimen brought to you."

"Sir, yes, sir!" Liz James gave a parody of a salute and marched from the nav deck, her face red.

"Do you find it necessary to alienate people?" asked Indira Smith softly.

"I find it necessary to establish discipline," he said coldly. "Clearly, there was not enough of it in the Terran Disaster Corps."

Conrad was angry. Experience had taught him that anger—like love and hate—was a dangerous emotion. It clouded a man's judgment. Experience had also taught him that the best remedy was work. He went to his cabin to bring the log up to date and to work out a programme of exploration.

As he settled down to the paper work, he began to grow calmer. He realised that his anger had been triggered not so much by the attitudes of James and Smith as by the loss of one valuable robot so soon after touch-down. He blamed himself. His instructions should have been more precise. The loss was unnecessary. There was plenty of sophisticated electronic equipment aboard the *Santa Maria*. He should have had the robots checking ground support with every step they took . . .

During the next three days, everyone worked hard at their assignments and at getting themselves into good physical condition. With some satisfaction, Conrad noted that they worked harder than he required—particularly the three women. It was as if they were going flat out to prove to him that they were talented and responsible people who didn't need a commander with a Napoleon complex. All of which suited Conrad fine. In this kind of operation, he thought, it didn't matter whether or not they liked him. All that mattered was that they should give their best.

Liz James and Chantana Le Gros established beyond all possible doubt that the bio-specimens they had examined functioned on an Earth-norm carbon cycle. Which meant simply that the life-forms of Kratos discovered so far—though they were structured differently from Terran life forms—operated on the same principle. The plants used CO_2 and built it into organic compounds, and the animals released CO_2 in their oxygenation process. The robots had brought in five small animals for analysis. Two were similar to terrestrial rats, one was strikingly like a grey squirrel, one was similar to a rabbit or hare, and one had most of the characteristics of a common grass snake. They were all relatively harmless.

Towards dusk on the second day, Fidel Batista, still doing most of the monitoring, thought he saw on the screen something massive in the middle distance. Unfortunately, video-recording had been suspended at the end of the first day to conserve tape for visual record of the team's progress; so no playback was possible. And, as luck would have it, no robots were working outside the vessel at the time. So Conrad had to rely only on Batista's impressions, which were not too helpful.

He claimed he had seen something very long that moved with a rippling motion. But, within a second or two, it had passed out of sight, probably moving on to low ground. If darkness had not been imminent, Conrad would have sent a couple of robots to investigate. But he did not wish to risk any more losses.

Looking at Batista's tired eyes, red-rimmed from staring, he decided that quite possibly the man had seen something that simply was not there. He remembered the time when he himself had had to take a long spell of duty on watch when two senior officers were sick during a shoot to Mars. He had been gazing through the observation panel—not because he needed to but because he wanted to—for about a couple of hours, when he thought he saw the sun-side of another vessel on collision course with his own.

He had been a one-stripe lieutenant at the time and was only on his fifth shoot. He had hit the Emergency button and got the master, groggy with flu, on the nav deck before he thought to check with radar. Radar showed nothing on the screens. And sub-lieutenant Conrad earned himself a severe reprimand. But the vessel had seemed real enough at the time . . .

"O.K. Fidel, I'll buy it. You saw something. How long had you been on duty?"

"Three hours, maybe. I can't remember."

"Then how the hell can you remember what you

saw?" demanded Conrad. "No. Scrub that. I'll take your word. But the light was poor and you were tired. There's a margin for error, isn't there?"

"If you say so, Commander."

"I do say so. At first light tomorrow, I'll send a couple of robots out. What did you say the range was?"

"About two thousand metres, roughly north-west."

"Well, then, let's put it on ice till tomorrow."

But when daylight came and the robots went out no trace could be found in the area indicated by Fidel Batista. But about five hundred metres farther away there was a long deep rut in the ground. It was impossible to determine whether or not the rut was of recent origin.

The morning was warm and fine—like a spring morning in southern Europe, thought Conrad, maybe Italy or Spain. Despite the loss of Paul, Conrad was feeling vaguely optimistic. He decided that he had been driving his team too hard, both in terms of work and in terms of discipline. Perhaps now was the time for a little relaxation. According to his earlier decree, they were not to venture forth on the surface of Kratos until day four. But Base One was virtually ready for occupation. The robots had completed the erection of the perimeter fence, which consisted of steel net, now wired via a step-up transformer to the *Santa Maria*'s generator. The electrified fence carried one thousand volts at low amperage—enough to discourage any would-be intruder without killing it stone dead. And, of course, the power could be immediately increased if any of the indigenous life-forms decided to get aggressive.

After an early breakfast, consisting of genuine coffee and genuine toast and marmalade, taken in his own cabin, Conrad went to the nav deck. He found Lieutenant Smith monitoring the screens.

"Anything to report?" he asked.

"Yes, Commander. The sun is above the horizon, the grass is green, the day is warm. Birds are on the wing, and the butterflies of Kratos don't care a shit about the sinister Terran invasion."

He chose to ignore the hostility in her voice. "So go out and enjoy it all," he said evenly. "You and James and Le Gros have been working pretty hard in the lab. Go get some sunshine."

She looked at him incredulously. "According to the master plan, I thought we weren't to face the great unknown until tomorrow."

He grinned. "The master plan has been slightly modified. Commander's privilege. But don't go outside the perimeter, not yet. O.K.?"

"Thank you." Her voice had softened. She turned to go.

"Oh, Lieutenant."

"Yes, sir?"

"How's Kwango?"

"No rejection symptoms. No infection. He's picking up strength."

"Fine. Do I still have to go through sterility procedure when I visit him?"

She thought for a moment or two. "Probably not. But I would prefer another six or seven days. He's my patient, and I would rather be over-cautious than sorry."

"You're the boss . . . In a sense, you and the rest of the team are my patients, too, Lieutenant. I also would rather be over-cautious than sorry."

She turned back and faced him. "I'm afraid I've been difficult. You are right about discipline, of course."

"Cancel statement," he said lightly. "I regret I had to play the heavy. Cancel that statement also . . . Lieutenant Smith, fresh out of S.A. you disobeyed orders and earned a reprimand. You also coped brilliantly with an emergency and earned a citation. Both are entered in the log, and that is all there is to it."

Indira smiled at him. It was the first time she had smiled at him for days. "James Conrad, you are a very difficult man."

He grinned. "That seems to be a majority verdict. Now get the hell out of this tin can. There are flowers out there that look like the dog-daisies I knew as a boy. I would not greatly object if somebody picked a bunch for my cabin. O.K.?"

"O.K., Commander."

FLASH SIX

Departure

At Kennedy, they saw the ground-to-orbit vessel that would take them up to the F.T.L. ship already inserted in the two-hour orbit, one thousand and forty miles above the surface of the Earth.

The ferry vessel was a slender metal column three hundred metres high. It could lift one hundred and fifty tons of payload. It would have to. Besides taking the Expendables to a rendezvous in the two-hour orbit, it would have to take seven exo-skeletons, six robots, fourteen space suits, seven suspended animation units, two one-man choppers, an armoured hovercar, seismic survey equipment, ten tons of conventional explosives, fifty tons of water, one ton of assorted weapons, seven tons of tools, equipment and spares, twelve tons of conventional food, food concentrates and medical supplies, one ton of personal effects, and the components for one incredibly small matter receiver.

Conrad surveyed the ship professionally. The rest of the team gazed at it in awe. It was the first time any of them had seen a space-ship at close quarters.

"It's beautiful," said Liz James. "I had no idea that

spaceships were so beautiful. You see them on the vid, but somehow the beauty is lost."

"This one is an old hulk," said Conrad professionally. "Its days are numbered. But, I agree, it's still beautiful. It is called *The Golden Hind*. I commanded it once . . . But that is a long time ago . . ." His voice trailed off, and he gazed at the ship with a bemused expression.

"I have read your file, too," said Lieutenant Smith softly. "You took *The Golden Hind* to Mercury, overloaded with emergency equipment because the colony's recycling systems had begun to fail. Legend has it that you hit the auto-pilot with a hammer, assumed manual control and clipped almost one hundred hours off the projected voyage time, thereby saving many lives. Wasn't that when they gave you the D.S.S.C.?"

"Lieutenant, you read too much. It's a bad habit." He laughed. "Legend is wrong. Being paranoid, I suspected a malfunction in the nav-computer and short-circuited it with a spanner. I was lucky. It was a hunch that paid off. Now let's hurry. We have to get processed by the medics, sign claim waivers, dispose of unwanted personal effects, empty our bowels and sweat all the surplus fluid out of our bodies in the sauna. It all takes longer than you think."

"Boss, when do we get chilled?" asked Kurt Kwango.

"Foreknowledge will improve your state of mind?" enquired Conrad.

"I'm a Buddhist. I need time for meditation."

Conrad glanced at his watch. "Meditate while you are sweating in the sauna, Kurt. We have a strict schedule. About six hours from now we will all be in suspended animation."

Chantana Le Gros shuddered. "Is it necessary for us to be sealed up while we are still on Earth?"

"Yes, Madame Le Gros, it is. The medicos don't like to use S.A. techniques in free fall if they can avoid it. Apart from the cost of taking all their equipment and personnel into space, there are technical problems."

"So we go to bye-byes on Earth and wake up—if we are lucky—on Kratos?" enquired Lou Andreas.

"You will be taken out of S.A. before we touch down," promised Conrad. "The resuscitation procedures take time. You'll be as weak as a kitten when you come out of S.A. You have to get strong again before we hit Kratos."

"Madre de Dios," observed Fidel Batista. "At least in S.A. my bum won't hurt."

EVENT SEVEN

Things That Go Bump in the Night

Day eleven, Kratos time. Conrad noted the salient facts in his log. Kwango was operational once more. Still rather weak, but available for light duty. Which was a big help. While convalescent, he had kept up with the results of the analysis of bio-samples; and from the vast quantity of data supplied—yet still minute from an ecologist's point of view—he was busy developing possible ecological scenarios. One of his more confident predictions was that substantial deposits of coal would eventually be discovered, as well as petroleum. If that turned out to be true, thought Conrad, the settlers on Kratos would have it made.

A lot of work had been done in eleven days. Apart from robot help, Lou Andreas had, almost single-handed, assembled the components of three exo-skeletons and had given Liz James and Fidel Batista a crash-course in their basic use.

The exo-skeletons had this much in common with robots: they were anthropomorphic machines, atomically powered. But, unlike the robots, they did not have independent control systems. The robots had their own "brains" and recourse to the master "brain" of Matthew. They were man-sized and they could accept human commands or function independently of man. The exoskeletons were eight metres long from feet to control crown and, without a man or woman in the control harness, they were useless junk.

But with skilled operators in harness, they were formidable. They could do the work of bulldozers, cranes, excavators. They could run across the countryside at 70 k.p.h., build roads, dig ditches, pluck up trees and, in effect, do anything that an eight-metre giant with the power of fifty men could do. The exo-skeletons, once the team had been trained to operate them efficiently, could be Conrad's equivalent of a construction gang of three hundred men or an armoured assault commando, as he chose. They were, he thought, his ultimate weapon for the taming of Kratos.

While Lou Andreas had been assembling the exoskeletons, Conrad himself had been busy. He had assigned Matthew and Mark to rig the *Santa Maria*'s discharge derrick and swing one of the choppers and the armoured hovercar out of the vessel's hold, through the now opened hatchway and down to ground. He had then assigned Lieutenant Smith to medium-range reconnaissance in the hovercar while he undertook aerial survey in the chopper.

Indira Smith was instructed to explore an area within five kilometre's radius of Base One. Conrad himself proposed to survey the terrain extending to a radius of twenty kilometres.

Between them, they made many interesting discoveries. Indira found two streams and a river. Fish abounded. She took samples of the water and of the river life. Some of the fish proved to be edible, tasting like trout. But one small, harmless-looking fish—reminiscent of the Terran carp—turned out to be lethally poisonous. A mouthful would kill a human being within the hour. Lieutenant Smith also examined the nearest network of ruts. She found that they were almost one metre deep and two metres wide. They looked freshly made. The soil and clay were clearly exposed; and the plant life in the ruts was sparse and small.

But it was Conrad who made the most enigmatic discovery. He found an artificial hill. At least, it looked like an artificial hill. It was perfectly circular, smoothly dome-shaped. But from the base, spiralling up to the apex, was one long, smooth, deep rut. In contrast to the rich profusions of trees, shrubs, ferns and grasses of the surrounding countryside, there was little vegetation on the hill's surface—chiefly patches of short grass and what appeared to be lichen. The hill rose about nine hundred metres above its immediate environs. Conrad circled it several times at different altitudes, fascinated. He photographed it from all angles, increasing magnification systematically. The prints dropped out of the camera's processing unit at the rate of one every ten seconds.

Finally, he decided to touch down near the base of the hill. He cut the chopper's engine and waited for silence. Then he picked up a laser rifle and climbed out of the plasti-glass control bubble. He felt the warm wind on his face, and it felt good. He stood still, listening, looking. He felt/heard a faint beating/throbbing. He felt it through the soles of his boots more than he heard it through his ears. It seemed to emanate from the hill. He looked at it closely, almost expecting it to pulsate. There was no visible movement, yet the beating/throbbing continued. It was as if the hill contained a monstrous and irregularly beating heart. He stood quite still, listening to and feeling the throb for several minutes. Then he got back into the chopper and lifted off.

He circled the enigmatic hill once more, greatly troubled. The symmetry of the thing and the perfectly carved spiral rut indicated that it had been constructed —but by what kind of creature and for what purpose? On preliminary investigation, Kratos had seemed to be a world almost ideally suited for colonisation. But if it contained creatures capable of creating a dome nine hundred metres high, the problems of colonisation could be formidable. One thing seemed certain to Conrad: the structure could not have been created by a race of pygmies—not unless they had atomic energy. The thing was bigger—far bigger—than any of the pyramids of Egypt. The species that had constructed it must have tremendous power at their disposal. Which would make them dangerous adversaries of man.

Presumably, these were the creatures which had made the ruts/roads/tracks/communication networks over much of the planet's land area. If so, judging from the extent of their operations, it would be a long time before man could challenge their supremacy. Yet why had they not yet shown themselves? If they were intelligent creatures, surely they would have noted the arrival of the *Santa Maria,* and surely they would have tried to establish contact or, more probably, destroy the invaders?

Conrad returned to Base One in a sombre mood. He

was unimpresstd by the fact that James and Batista, in their exo-skeletons, could now play ball with each other, throwing and catching rocks that weighed fifty kilos.

"Why so glum, Commander?" enquired Lieutenant Smith. "The programme goes well, and you can have genuine Kratos trout for supper."

He thrust the photo prints into her hands. "Take a look at these goddamned things."

She looked, and took the implications in at a glance. "Trouble?"

"Trouble. The jokers who put up that little edifice are either very massive creatures or they have great energy sources. Take your pick."

"I have taken my pick," she said calmly. "They are massive creatures."

"I'll tell you something else," said Conrad. "The bloody hill is alive. I touched down at its base. And I felt and heard something that seemed like a fantastic and irregular heartbeat."

Lieutenant Smith raised an eye-brow, but she made no comment.

"It was so powerful," went on Conrad. "that I could feel it through the ground."

"Was there any opening anywhere?"

He shrugged. "You've seen the prints."

"What about the base, or the nearby ground?"

"There didn't seem to be any opening round the base. I didn't stay long enough for any more investigation." He shrugged, then added drily, "I only had one laser rifle, and it didn't seem a good idea to risk you having to assume command so soon."

"What next?"

"We'll have to investigate, of course. The planet looks damn near perfect for colonisation; but we can't have any mysteries—at least not of this magnitude. We have to find out about the ruts and about the bloody dome, and assess the potential of hostile life-forms."

"Must alien life-forms necessarily be hostile to us?"

"Survival of the fittest," he said laconically. "Take it from me, that is a cosmic constant. Also, Lieutenant, something tells me that people who assume that alien life-forms are hostile live longer than those who don't."

She smiled. "You are right. Two dozen Kratos trout didn't have any opinion at all about alien life-form. I lasered them as they swam. How do you like yours, hot or cold?"

"Save the funnies," he snapped with some irritation. "There are six or seven hours of daylight left. During that time I want the perimeter defences strengthened. All hands—including me and the robots—are going to set up another perimeter fence three metres from this one, and three metres high. We'll connect them both with criss-cross nylon rope, so that if anything does choose to ignore the voltage, it will probably strangle itself trying to get through. In the next few days, when more people can operate the exo-skeletons efficiently, we'll use some of the local timber and construct a good old-fashioned stockade inside the perimeter."

"I didn't know you were as worried as that," she said.

"Well, now you do. The robots can get cracking immediately while the rest of us grab something to eat." He took a small transceiver out of the big thigh-pocket of his fatigue trousers. "Matthew, do you read me?"

"I read you, sir."

Matthew was only about seventy metres away, inside the perimeter, drilling a small-bore well with a hypersonic lance. Seismic survey had revealed that there was water about seventy-five metres below ground level. And since the water of Kratos was, according to analysis, just as good as the water of Terra, Conrad had thought it sensible to hook in to the local supply as soon as possible and thus reduce the load on the *Santa Maria*'s recycling system.

"Priority decision, countermanding previous decisions. All robots will disengage from non-vital assignments. They will draw from stores sufficient tensile steel wire and support duralumin angle girders to erect a second perimeter fence three metres high and three metres beyond the first. The gateway will be parallel to gateway one and of the same proportions. Execute."

"Decision noted, sir. Execution proceeds."

"That means we have to get our own lunch," said Indira lightly.

"Yes," said Conrad. "One of the sad hardships of planet-taming. Tell the others. They have thirty minutes to prepare, eat and digest. After that we see whether mere humans can lick the robots for speed and efficiency."

The second fence was up and hooked in to the generator before nightfall. Conrad was amazed. He hadn't really thought it could be done. He was even more amazed when he saw Kurt Kwango hefting a thirty-kilo coil of nylon rope to the perimeter.

"I thought you were only available for light duty, Kwango. That was the last report I got from Lieutenant Smith."

"Report cancelled, Massa Boss. Dis little old nigra fit for anything."

"Kurt, you are a stupid bastard."

"It takes one to know one—sir."

Conrad laughed. He reflected that back on Terra he would probably have punished Kwango for insolence. But here on Kratos the notion of punishment for such a triviality seemed irrelevant. Besides, during Kwango's convalescence, Conrad had got to know him pretty well. He thought he had begun to understand what made Kwango tick. He was afraid of himself. The history of violence revealed a deep insecurity. And because of that, Kwango, being a proud man, saw everything and everyone as a personal challenge.

But there was something else—something in the way he had said the words that translated them into a declaration of friendship, or loyalty, or both.

"You have the advantage, Kurt," he said evenly. "You are a stupid black bastard, I am merely a stupid white one."

It was Kwango's turn to laugh. "Excuse me, Commander. I got work to do. I got to help rig your mouse-trap so you can sleep safe at nights." He swung the coil of nylon rope from one shoulder to the other and staggered to the perimeter. He was followed by one of the robots, John, effortlessly carrying three fifty-kilo coils of rope.

After the outer perimeter fence had been completed, Conrad ordered four searchlights to be set up on perimeter quadrant points, each searchlight to swing regularly through one hundred and eighty degrees, the beams parallel with the surface of Kratos and one point five metres above ground level. Throughout the hours of darkness, one robot would monitor the screens on the nav deck while another, armed with a laser rifle, patrolled the perimeter. The robot on the screens was instructed to rouse Conrad only if the lights revealed any large animals in the vicinity. The robot on patrol was instructed to use his weapon only if the perimeter was in danger of being breached.

When the evening meal was over, Conrad called a conference in the saloon of tht *Santa Maria*. All the team was present. So was Matthew.

"Sit down, Matthew," said Conrad, gesturing to a vacant chair. "It makes me uncomfortable to see you standing."

"Sir, the saloon chairs are designed for human use. They may not support my weight, which is two hundred and seven point five kilos, Earth-G."

"Then sit on the deck, damn you."

"Decision noted. Execution proceeding. Query term 'damn-you'." Matthew's voice was imperturbable.

"Cancel term!" snapped Conrad. Matthew plonked himself down with all the grace of a dying elephant. The deck shook.

Liz James giggled. "One of these days, when I feel like wrecking the joint, I'll teach him how to dance the polka."

Conrad ignored her. "We have a problem. You all know what it is. So far, Kratos has obliged us by seeming to be a friendly planet. The animals, insects, birds, fish we have discovered have all been small and, with one or two exceptions, pretty harmless. But, as of now, the honeymoon period is over. You are already familiar with the network of ruts, and you have seen the shots I took of the artificial hill, itself covered by a spiral rut.

My conclusion is that the ruts and the hill are the work of some creature, formidable in size and strength and maybe formidable in intelligence. Does anyone challenge that conclusion?"

There was silence for a few moments. Then Liz James said: "I'm the biologist, so the ball seems to be in my court. I agree, Commander, that the evidence suggests the existence of some large creature. On Earth termites and ants can construct hills. True, they are not big compared to the one you found. But in relation to the size of the termites or ants, they are colossal monuments. On Kratos, despite some similarities between the indigenous life-forms and terrestrial life-forms, we cannot afford to rely on conventional criteria. I agree that your hill could have been raised by very large creatures; but it is also possible that relatively small life-forms—given sufficient numbers and a group programming—could have carried out the task." She shrugged, then smiled. "I merely open the field for possibilities."

"Thank you, Liz," said Conrad. "But what about the throbbing I felt when I stood near the hill."

"No comment," said Liz. "I'm baffled." Then she changed her mind. "But what if the hill contained a vast number of these creatures or insects, all doing the same thing—whatever it is—at the same time? That might produce the effect you experienced."

"Like a regiment of infantry marching over a bridge without breaking step?" enquired Conrad.

"Something like that."

"Not on. I can't tell you why it's not on, but I know it. Also there are the ruts to consider."

Kwango flashed a broad smile. "May I make some contribution to the discussion?"

"Go ahead, Kurt. We need ideas."

"First, may I point out that I have some slight advantage over the rest of you. I have lived in Africa. Not just the Africa of cities and super cities. The old Africa. The Africa of forest and bush and desert. Shall I tell you, Commander, why you have seen no big game?"

"Enjoy yourself, Kurt." It was Fidel Batista speaking. "Reveal all. We have a high respect for your intelligence." He stroked his buttock tenderly. "You are the man who jumped in with the sharks because he couldn't make it with a girl."

There was general laughter.

Kwango rose above it. "The reason is like now," he announced calmly. "You make too much goddamn noise. Consider, first this tin can comes falling out of the sky with sonic booms, rockets roaring and whatever. Then the good Commander lets the robots play boy scouts, knocking poles in the ground and stringing up pretty wires. And if that wasn't enough, he had them doing it all over again. We got a whining hovercar, a chopper that makes a sound like a house falling down, five half-ton robots square-dancing on command, and Lou teaching the children how to operate exo-skeletons and play ball with fifty-kilo rocks ... Brothers and sisters, that is one hell of a lot of noise."

"Kurt, I believe you have a point," said Conrad.

"Sure as dammit, I have," said Kwango. "I got several points. In my country even the stupid ones know that big game is more nervous than small game. I'm only surprised that, while I was taking my siesta, you managed to collect any bio-samples at all. They must have been so deaf or so crazed they didn't care any more. So, while you have been playing with wire and throwing rocks around and making enough noise to scare the shit out of any intelligent animals in the vicinity, the big creatures have pissed off, as de poet says, to fresh woods and pastures new."

"I'll buy that," said Conrad. "But what about my bloody hill?"

"Commander, I was coming to that," said Kwango in a pained voice. "While you people been running round the country-side and scaring the game away, I have been doing some thinking. About the ruts. Item, apart from where they cross each other they do not have any angles. Item, careful analysis—my careful analysis—of the pix show that the ruts have a slightly but regular unevenness. Item, the concealed hole the robot fell down is exactly the same diameter as the ruts. Item, the Commander's hill has a spiral rut running from apex to base. Item, no creature has yet been observed using or making the ruts. Item, this planet has no moon, therefore the nights are always pretty dark . . . Children, before I spring the big surprise, indulge my quaint humour. What has twenty-two yellow legs and two wings?"

He was met by blank looks.

"Kwango, come to the point," said Conrad wearily. "We have no time for bumper fun book stuff."

"Then you should make time, Commander, sir. The brain needs to be exercised as well as the body. A Chinese football team has twenty-two yellow legs and two wings. See? Something you wouldn't think of."

"Oh, my God!" said Liz James.

Kwango was enjoying himself. "Now, I solve your mystery. The noise we made coming down out of the sky and then setting up this so-called security perimeter drove away all the big intelligent creatures. Except the ones that couldn't afford to migrate because they had built themselves a nice air-conditioned home which, for the sake of convenience, I now call Mount Conrad.

"Your hill, Commander, is the nest of a colony of nocturnal, omnivorous snake-like creatures. The computer and me both agree that, fully grown, they are some three metres in diameter at the widest point, that they are about ninety metres long, that they have a capability of moving rapidly—say fifty kilometres an hour flat out, that they each weigh approximately three hundred tons Earth norm, and that they are not very nice people. Message ends."

There was silence. Everyone looked at Kurt Kwango.

Lou Andreas said: "Kwango, you are full of crap."

Liz James said carefully: "It is just possible. But it is one hell of a leap into the dark."

Chantana Le Gros smiled. "Mr. Kwango has had his fun. Quite entertaining. Personally, I enjoyed the performance."

"It fits," said Conrad heavily. "By Jesus, it fits . . . It's a tall one but—has anyone else got a more sensible offer?"

No one had.

"Then let's hit the sack. It has been a long day. Tomorrow, we will try to find out whether Kurt's twenty-two yellow legs and two wings really belong to a Chinese football team."

Conrad slept badly. He had nightmares. Oddly, they were not about a hill full of super-colossal snakes.

They were about a doomed ship falling into the sun. About the men who had lost their lives, trying to take off her crew. About a smashed and withered arm. About an eye that had virtually melted in its socket when the phototropic visor of Conrad's space-suit had packed up. About the intolerable torrent of radiation that poured out from that vast globe of an atomic furnace that was trying to suck two space ships into its fiery heart.

In the middle of the night, there were other nightmares. But these were for real. Because they happened when Matthew hit the general alarm button on the nav deck. Conrad didn't wait for verbal explanation on the intercom. He shook the sleep out of his one normal eye and the other nightmare out of his head, and rushed— half naked—up to the nav deck.

Lieutenant Smith had beaten him to it. She, too, was half-naked, her prosthetic legs looking like chiselled marble beneath her short night-tunic.

The party was almost over. Two of the searchlights had already been knocked out. The great roars and thuds that came over the audio were sickening, awe-inspiring, terrifying—as were the great indistinct shapes that threshed about on the perimeter, shaking the ground and even the *Santa Maria* herself.

Conrad stared, fascinated, at the screens. Matthew was giving an appreciation in his cold, logical way, of the events as they occurred. But, somehow, the words did not register. It didn't matter. Conrad could get the playback—verbatim—later. All that mattered now was what was happening on the screens.

He saw monstrous serpentine shapes, threshing about on the perimeter. A beam of light caught one as it reared, showing the glistening, fantastic and segmented body. Another shattering roar, then the third searchlight died. The remaining one swept to and fro crazily as if it was being held by a drunkard. Its beam showed briefly a dreadful head, decapitated by the wires and nylon ropes of the defence system.

The face—if you could call it that—was fully two metres in diameter. The mouth, wide open, was a black chasm—large enough to take in four men side by side. The seven eyes—if they were eyes—were spaced at regular intervals in a half-moon shape close over the thick, top, obscene lip of the cavernous mouth. They reflected the searchlight beam, shining briefly like grotesque stars.

There was yet another great roar, and the last searchlight was smashed.

Lieutenant Smith sank on her haunches, retching. By then the rest of the team had arrived on the nav deck. Kwango, the rapist, the brilliant ecologist, knelt by Lieutenant Smith, stroked her back, held her gently as she vomited.

Conrad wiped the sweat from his forehead.

"Ladies and gents," he said, as calmly as he could, "we have now discovered the nature of the opposition. It is a great step forward."

Chantana Le Gros laughed. "It seems more like a great step backwards. Why didn't we pull out while the going is good and declare the planet unfit for colonisation?"

"Because we are Expendables," said Conrad with sudden ferocity. "Because it is our job to prove this planet one way or the other, not to get the shit scared out of us by things that go bump in the night. Because it cost a billion solars to put us here. That money—as Lieutenant Smith will be the first to tell you—could have been spent on land reclamation projects, on schools, hospitals, hydroponics farms for a worn-out planet that has too many people. But U.N. chose to gamble on us and on the possibility of a new world. There are Indian, Chinese, South American children now dying of starvation because of the billion solars it took to get us to Kratos. You want them to die for no reason? I don't . . . We are all social trash, one way or another. So it doesn't really matter a damn whether *we* live or die. Except that on the other side of the sky there are people who backed us, gave us what we needed, and are now waiting patiently for results. We are going to give them the results—at least, the survivors are. O.K.?"

"O.K. Commander." It was Lou Andreas who spoke. He gave a faint smile. "It was a great commercial. I'm sold on the packaging. Personally, I think we are now going to have to concentrate on the exo-training."

"Great minds think alike," said Conrad drily.

"Commander, I appeal on de grounds of racial discrimination," said Kwango in his best Uncle Tom voice. "It appears I'm still carrying de white man's burden."

"What the hell are you talking about?"

Kurt grinned. "You white trash only got to face de prospect of dying once. For dis pore, ignorant black man, it's de second time around."

Suddenly, the tension broke. And everyone was laughing.

The Secrets
of
Kratos

PHASE ONE

Investigation: Death's Head

Conrad went out at first light. He took Andreas and Batista with him. They wore heavy, armoured jackets. They carried laser rifles. Among other things, they were looking for the robot John, who had been patrolling the perimeter, also armed with a laser rifle, during the attack.

Throughout the rest of the night, no one had slept. Batista had spent some of the time arming half a dozen of his favourite toys—cold nitro bombs. They were vacuum insulated steel spheres containing solid nitroglycerine. The arming device was his own invention. Set the electronic fuse timing, throw the bomb; and, after the required interval, instant heat would be applied to the nitro-glycerine. Bang!

Batista's speciality was not needed. The attackers had gone. But they had left behind them trails of devastation, one certain casualty, and one robot literally flattened into the ground.

John's duralumin-clad control centre had been crushed as if it were silver paper. His steel limbs were distorted. He lay in a rut that was fully two metres deep.

"Where the hell is his laser?" said Conrad. It could not be found; maybe it was under him.

"These creatures play real rough," said Andreas. "They can make one hell of a mess of expensive equipment."

Batista fingered one of his cold nitro bombs lovingly. "I wish one would show its ugly head just now. I'd like to see how it reacts to a half-litre of nitro."

"A head, we already have," observed Conrad, pointing to the grotesque and horrifying thing that lay tangled in the wreckage of the perimeter wire. "I wonder what happened to the rest of the body? Did its friends somehow drag it away, or did they eat it? It's a pity the searchlights were put out so soon . . . Well, thank goodness we haven't had any breakfast yet. Let's go take a close look, gentlemen. I'm not surprised Lieutenant Smith threw up. Even from here, it looks godawful."

From close up, the head was worse than horrific. It was obscene, repulsive in a way that could not be defined.

The mouth, frozen in the rictus of death, had thick grey lips that looked as if they were made of foamed latex. They were covered in a very regular fashion with pustules—or were they suckers? Suckers that might clamp on to prey struggling to escape. The lips, more than thirty centimetres thick, seemed fixed in a wide and horrible grin, as if the creature had died laughing. There were no teeth in the mouth. Evidently, the creature did not need to masticate. But there were four tight coils of muscular tissue. One at each side of the orifice, one centered on the top jaw and one centred on the bottom. Tongues or some kind of tentacles? Conrad surmised that they might have a function similar to the tentacles of an octopus or squid. Perhaps they could flash out, snatch the prey and draw it to the suckers on the lips, where the unfortunate creature would be stuck prior to being swallowed whole.

"This bloody thing is segmented!" exclaimed Batista.

Conrad, who had been concentrating on the "face", took a look at the tissue behind the head, where the wires had cut into it, and where something had pulled the rest of the body away.

"It's like a worm," Conrad managed to say. Bile rose into his mouth. He tried very hard not to be sick. He succeeded, temporarily. "Apart from the face, it's like a king-size earthworm."

"Commander," said Andreas, "those things over the top lip are definitely eyes, Goddamit, this critter has got to be the most shit-awful thing that ever existed."

Also it stank. And the gaping wound where the head had been torn from the body oozed. Gobbits of brown semi-solid body matter, covered with a mass of slime and mucus, still tumbled out from the already rotting head.

Conrad forced himself to step over the tangle of perimeter wire and go behind the dreadful thing. And look.

He was utterly appalled at what he saw. The four metres of head section was almost hollow. The mass on the ground was only a small portion of the flesh that should have been there. The rest had been gouged out, presumably devoured.

"The problem of the missing body has been solved," he said unsteadily. "They didn't drag it away. They ate it."

Then he lost the battle with his stomach and began to vomit. Andreas and Batista were wise enough to leave him alone, to look the other way.

After he had stopped retching, Andreas said gently: "Look, skipper. This damn thing is getting me. I don't feel too good. Why don't we go back to the *Santa Maria* and get ourselves some strong black coffee? Batista ain't too happy, either—are you, Fidel?"

Fidel Batista laughed grimly. "That, my friend, is some understatement. I, personally, would like to scream somewhat. I am prevented only by the fact that I represent the people of Cuba in this terrible place."

When he had finished being sick, Conrad said: "O.K. I take the point. You are being kind, and I appreciate it. Now, come over here and see what I have seen."

Batista was sick first. He beat Andreas by all of two seconds.

"Now, you know," said Conrad tranquilly. "Now, we'll go get that coffee."

Aboard the *Santa Maria*, their spirits recovered somewhat. But when one of the robots brought Andreas his favourite breakfast of ham and eggs he had to rush from the saloon. Conrad and Batista were wiser. Their breakfast consisted entirely of black coffee.

The others joined them in the saloon. Surprisingly,

Lieutenant Smith ate well. So did Kwango. But Chantana Le Gros and Liz James stuck with coffee and toast.

After breakfast, Conrad held a brief council of war. All the Expendables were present, as was Matthew.

Conrad wasted no time. "Kurt was right about the nature of the opposition. Give the man a cigar. But as of now, we must stop thinking of these creatures in Earth-terms. Snake-like, wormlike—it doesn't bloody matter. They are simply big, fast moving creatures that appear to have great strength and every repulsive characteristic in the book. There are two major questions to be answered. The first is: are they a common species or a rare one? Were we just plain unlucky touching down near one of their nests, or would we have encountered them if we had touched down anywhere on Continent B? If they are as rare as the elephants—or whales —of Terra, we have a chance of licking them. If they are as common as rabbits in Australia, we might as well wrap it up with a negative report on colonisation potential."

"Unless," said Kwango, "we can combat them with a kind of myxomatosis, as with the Australian rabbits."

"A possibility," agreed Conrad, "but a long-range one. We don't have the resources or the time to develop synthetic diseases. Though that need not stop us trying. The value of such a project will have to be determined by the experts, Le Gros and James. Anyway, a priority task is to determine how abundant these creatures are."

"I can tell you now that they are not very abundant," said Kurt Kwango authoritatively. "To support a mass of three hundred tons, those bastards need a hell of a lot of food—proteins, carbohydrates, fats."

"You said they are omnivorous."

Kwango shrugged. "Also, it seems, cannibalistic—which proves that they need a lot of food."

Conrad cleared his throat. "We can answer the first question by simple survey. I will take the chopper, Lieutenant Smith will take the hovercar. And we will both survey a block of one million square kilometers. The incidence of nests—or hives or whatever—should give the computer enough data to provide extrapolations. That's fairly easy, routine. To answer the second question is going to be more difficult. I want to know if these creatures are intelligent. There are two ways to find out; by observing the living and analysing the dead. We don't have any living specimens just now—thank God—but there's a fragment of dead horror down in our own backyard. James and Le Gros, find out as much as you can from it." He gave a thin smile. "I ought to warn you. It won't be nice. I recommend you use the sealed clothing and bottled air we have for inspection of the hot deck. I recommend also that you follow decontamination procedure afterwards."

"Don't worry, Commander," said Liz James. "We won't be sick—provided we can use a couple of robots."

"I see . . . I have only four robots left—which is one hell of a wastage, considering how long we have been here. I was planning to use all four to help build a new defence system. How long would you need the robots for?"

"Two hours, maybe three."

"You can have one robot for three hours. Matthew assign one of your brethren to assist Miss James and Miss Le Gros."

"Query term brethren, sir?"

"Cancel bloody term," snapped Conrad. "Execute!"

"Decision noted, sir. Execution proceeds. Mark assigned. Unless orders are countermanded, he will now prepare two suits, sealed clothing, two bottles oxygen-nitrogen standard Earth ratio."

Conrad ignored him. "How do you feel, Kwango?"

Kwango grinned. "Bloody O.K. Commander, sir. *I* ate a good breakfast. Want me to tell you about it?"

"Spare me the details, funny man. You have work to do." He turned to Lou Andreas. "Think you can train this black genius to use an exo-skeleton in a couple of hours?"

Andreas scratched his head. "Don't rightly know, Boss. I met these genius types before." He grinned. "Shit-hot when it comes to the big think, but on the practical matters of life, they are just like babies."

Conrad was in no mood for further banter. "Do it," he said. "Because you and her and the robots have a particularly important assignment. You are going to build a stockade where the perimeter fence used to be. You are going to make it impregnable, so that if we get another visitation from those bastard things, they will do themselves considerable injury trying—and failing —to get through. They are big enough and tough enough to wreck the torus of the *Santa Maria*. If they are allowed to do that, we've had it."

"Where do we get the materials?"

"About two kilometres south of here, there is a large patch of tall trees with straight, slender trunks. From

the air, they look almost like Terrain pine trees. Anyway, that is your source of materials. Using the exo-
skeletons, you should be able to pluck them like dai-
sies. You will give the trunks sharp points and drive
them into the ground at an outward angle of, say, sixty
degrees. If you make the stockade about three metres
high, and those worms or snakes or whatever try to
slither over it, their own weight will cause them to im-
pale themselves. Right?"

"Right," agreed Andreas. He sighed. "But that is
going to be one hell of a job."

"You didn't come to Kratos for a rest cure," said
Conrad. "You came because you volunteered for hazardous duty, and you were chosen because you are socially expendable . . . O.K. We all have our assignments. Let's move."

Conrad's aerial survey revealed the existence of six
more dome-shaped hills in the block of one million
square kilometres. They all had the same characteristics as the first he had found, and they were almost
identical in size. The survey took two and a half days.
Lieutenant Smith confirmed his findings and also made
another interesting discovery. She found one of the
creatures whole and dead. There was no mark upon it,
no apparent reason for its death. She measured it, took
photographs and samples from each segment of its fantastic body. These, together with the investigations carried out by James and Le Gros, yielded much-needed
information about what the Expendables came to call
the death worms.

In his survey, Conrad had not only discovered the
existence of more hives or nests, he had also seen much
animal life. Clearly, Kwango had been right. Most of

the animals had been scared away from the vicinity of the *Santa Maria* by the noise and disturbance of its touch-down. But, twenty or thirty kilometres away from the vessel, herds of game roamed the grasslands. Some of the animals looked amazingly like Terran deer, okapi, buffalo, eland, bison. If in fact Kratos were ever to be colonised, there would be no shortage of meat.

In the manipulation of an exo-skeleton, Kwango proved more adept than Andreas had anticipated. The stockade was completed in just over three days. Lou Andreas was proud of it. It was a formidable stockade. Between them, Andreas and Kwango had cleared three hectares of timber. And now the sharpened logs "planted" by the robots constituted a very tough barrier.

Strangely, Kwango had taken to the use of an exo-skeleton almost as the proverbial duck takes to water. He had needed far less instruction than either Batista or James. Once secured in his harness, it was as if he really felt the great machine to be an extension of his own body. At first, he had fallen down two or three times; but he learned from the falls and picked himself up. Soon, he was able to walk, leap, run. Soon he was as good as, or better than, Lou Andreas himself.

Andreas was somewhat mortified. Was there nothing that this black joker could not do? But he was very glad of Kwango's rapid learning of exo-skills when it came to trimming the "pine" logs and hauling them back to Base One. Kwango, without appearing to work unduly hard, somehow managed to deliver fifteen logs for every ten delivered by Andreas.

It was strange to see Kwango harnessed in eight

metres of pseudo-body loping—not walking—back to
Base One with two bundles of logs under his steel
arms. What was even more galling was the fact that
Kwango somehow made the exo-skeleton move gracefully.

The robots lasered the rough ends of the logs before
they were lowered into holes prepared by the sonic
drill. Kwango became adept at tossing the logs into
their holes as if he were flinging darts at a dartboard.

Conrad was pleased with the stockade. It looked a
very solid structure—tough enough not to get smashed
if there were any more nocturnal visits. He ordered
searchlights to be erected as before, and he had trip
wires linked to vid-cameras. If there was another visitation, he wanted a record that could be studied.

After the evening meal, he read the reports compiled
by Liz James and Chantana Le Gros. All they had to
go on was the messy stinking remains of the head; but
from that alone they had derived a remarkable amount
of information and had extrapolated high probabilities.

Most important of all was the fact that the creature
had a brain no larger than an orange—which clearly
ruled out high intelligence. Second, there was no evidence of any skeletal system—so it was more like a
king-size worm than a king-size snake. Third, it was,
as Kwango had suggested, an omnivore. James had
found traces of animal and vegetable matter in the
mouth. Fourth, the skin was a vast lung/excreting
mechanism. Fifth, it partially digested animal prey by
using jets of hydrochloric acid. Sixth, it was warm-
blooded. Seventh, its visual system was primitive in the
extreme. The eyes themselves would probably not respond to colour, only to light intensity and movement.

Conrad was tired. He had been doing a lot of work and a lot of thinking. But his brain refused to rest. So, before he went to his cabin, he challenged Kwango to a game of chess. He fully expected to lose. Kwango had a much higher I.Q.

So he started off with a king's pawn opening and developed his pieces as fast as he could. Kwango saw the attack on the king's side coming, and had his defences set up in advance.

"No good, Commander, think of something else." Kwango was smilingly happy. His next move was obviously to get the rooks into play, since Conrad had not yet castled.

Conrad sighed. It would have to be death or glory. He wasn't going to smash Kwango on chess logic.

He sacrificed a bishop, just for the hell of it. Kwango, confident as always, took it with the pawn in front of the king.

Conrad followed it up with a suicidal queen exchange. Kwango was laughing—until Conrad's knight bracketed king and rook.

"Shit!" said Kwango.

The black knight took the white rook and then was itself taken.

But the sequence of events had not only opened Kwango's defence, it had destroyed his attack. He began to develop his remaining pieces. But now he was one move behind and could only play a defensive game. Six moves later, Conrad was able to castle and double his rooks. Kwango protected his remaining rook with bishop and king. But, relentlessly, Conrad manoeuvred himself into position for a disclosed check. At which point, Kwango resigned.

"Commander, temperamentally you are a bloody kamikaze pilot. You have no subtlety, no elegance. But I know your style now. That is the last game you will win for a long time."

"No doubt," returned Conrad tranquilly. "I seem to recall that you played for Nigeria. So now you know my style, you will be able to smash me—but not always."

Kwango laughed. "Not always," he agreed. "Players like you sometimes produce rabbits out of hats."

Conrad was silent for a while. Then he said: "It was our first game, Kurt. You did not know my style nor I yours . . . In a way, we are faced with a similar situation here on Kratos."

"The worm-like creatures?"

"Precisely."

Kwango yawned. "I'm going to hit the sack. But before I do, there is something I should tell you. I don't think it was a good idea to use searchlights again."

"Why not?"

"Because I think those bastard things may be night creatures, and I think they may be phototropic. Like bloody moths."

"Have you any evidence to support this notion?"

"No. Except that they smashed all the lights on the first perimeter."

"Coincidence?"

"Possibly. I don't think so."

Conrad also yawned. "We'll see," he said.

They did see.

Later that night, the death worms came again. This time, they could not breach the perimeter defence. But they still managed to put out two of the lights. And five of their dreadful heads were left impaled upon the sharpened logs of the stockade.

The vid cameras recorded what happened to the massive bodies. The surviving death worms ate them. The odd thing was that the decapitated victims still struggled and threshed about, trying to defend themselves even as they were being devoured. It took a long time for them to die. The bodies continued to writhe until there were only three or four segments left. As he studied the playback, Conrad was reminded of the blood frenzy of sharks.

PHASE TWO

Battle Royal

Ecologist Kurt Kwango asked permission to deliver a brief lecture on extrapolations derived from analysis of the nature, and evidence of the behaviour, of what everyone called the death worms. He received permission. Conrad would have preferred a confidential report first; but he knew that Kwango was temperamental and liked to show off. High I.Q., brilliant mind—and the emotional instability of an adolescent. If Conrad had refused permission, it was a stone cold certainty that Kwango would have sulked, keeping his information to himself until he could find a sufficiently dramatic moment to reveal it.

Kwango surveyed his fellow Expendables benignly. "Are you sitting comfortably, children? Then I'll begin."

"Cut the crap," said Andreas. "You got a bad case of colonic verbalese."

"Some day, Lou," retorted Kwango with a note of insult in his voice, "you must allow me to teach you how to use an exo-skeleton efficiently." Kwango did not wait for any response, but turned his attention to the rest of the group.

"We have all been very busy recently, and a number of interesting facts about our charming, if aggressive, nocturnal visitors has been discovered. We are all familiar with the excellent analyses carried out by James, Le Gros, and the indefatigable Lieutenant Smith. Also, the good Commander has provided useful data about the incidence of the hives or nests of these creatures. As you know, I am an ecologist. The facts we have been given are like pieces of an old fashioned jig-saw puzzle. They have little significance until they are fitted together to make a picture. That is my job. I am a dedicated addict of jig-saw puzzles. It is my business to relate the functions and behaviour of our charming friends to the environment or eco-system in which they operate.

"Let us review the known facts. First, the robot probes brought to Terra sufficient data to convince the clever boys that Kratos was a planet that might be suitable for colonisation. They brought pictures of the networks of ruts, but they did not detect any animal life capable of creating them. Interesting. The robot probes did not orbit very long. I have checked the records and find that they orbited for only fourteen K-days.

"That is significant," went on Kwango. "Ladies and gentlemen, if some alien robot probe orbited Earth for fourteen days when the northern hemisphere was in the throes of winter, would the probe be able to provide useful data about the life cycle of, say, the Arctic seal in summertime?"

He paused dramatically. No one spoke. Conrad gazed at him intently. Kwango was gratified.

"The point is that the death worms of Kratos are anachronisms. They belong to much earlier geological ages—ages that might correspond to the Carboniferous or even perhaps as late as the Jurassic or Cretaceous periods on Earth. Consider the evidence.

"Much of the relatively small animal life forms we have found so far are comparable to creatures of Earth, and must have passed through similar phases of evolution. But the death worms! Ladies and gentlemen, it is as if on Terra the dinosaurs had survived through to the Pliocene or even the Pleistocene. They don't bloody belong!"

"So what, funny man," growled Lou Andreas, still smarting. "They are here. What the hell does it matter if they are not meant to be here? It's our job to annihilate the bastards if we can. Otherwise, no colonists. Kratos is a write-off."

"Lou is right," said Fidel Batista. "Your damned theorising is of no use, Kurt. What we want is the secret ingredient that makes them all go pop."

"You are both wrong," said Kwango loftily. "Our job is first to understand their function in the ecosystem and then see how we can neutralise their danger to man. Right, Commander?"

"Right, Mr. Kwango. Proceed. But justify this operation quickly. We all have work to do."

"You want the conclusions first or the reasoning?"

"The conclusions. If they are not crazy, you can then support your argument."

Kwango grinned. "Hokay, Boss. Fasten your seat belt. Like the dinosaurs of Earth, the dinosaurs of Kratos destroyed their own environment. Earth dinosaurs operated in humid swamps. But when they ate all the foliage off the plants, the swaps dried up. Bang went the dinosaurs. Of course, it took a few million years. Same thing happened here on Kratos. Only some of the dinosaurs—if you want to call them that—were stupidly smart. They changed their eating habits and they went underground. And because of that they managed to survive. But they didn't evolve. They devolved . . . So I'll just tell you what we got, man. And you can fire de sixty-four thousand solar questions later. We got a species that has two brains—one at each end—like some Terran dinosaurs. It's gone underground because it needs to create the humid conditions it once had. It is omnivorous, cannibalistic and regenerative. Cut one in two, and unless its best friend eats the sections, presently you got two death worms. These interesting creatures are phototropic and sensitive to heat stimulus. They stay in the hives or underground until conditions are right for their emergence to the surface. Then they come out and have a ball. We know that they breathe through their skin. Has anyone, other than me, been checking the rainfall and temperature readings lately?"

"My God, he's right!" Liz James sprang to her feet. "Kwango, I love you. You *are* a genius!"

"Darling, I love you also," said Kwango. "And it is self-evident that I am a genius. In this particular zone where the good Commander in his wisdom decided to touch down, we are about to enter the rainy season. What is the Terran word? Monsoon. Ah, yes. So, ladies and gentlemen, to put it briefly: you ain't seen nothing yet."

There was a silence. Then Conrad said: "Kurt, you really can back these extrapolations up?"

Kwango grinned. "Yep. You didn't know it, Boss, but you hired me to be the thinking man of this outfit."

"So it seems. Have you got any more bad news? If we are going to try to do anything about these creatures, we might as well know the worst."

"Yes, Commander, I have more bad news. I studied the pix you took of Mount Conrad. There were no entrances visible. Which indicates that the creatures are capable of subtlety. Why no entrances? Answer: entrances are concealed, probably at some distance from the nest. Why this, then? Answer: because the death worms fear attack. Attack from what? Other death worms . . . In fact, there is probably an entrance to that hill right here near our perimeter."

"The shaft the robot fell down," said Conrad.

"Score one, Commander. That shaft was carefully constructed. At the bottom, branching off, there is a tunnel, yes?"

"There is a tunnel," agreed Conrad.

"So. I bet anyone a litre of booze that it and any other nearby shafts lead to Mount Conrad."

There were no takers.

"To sum up," went on Kwango happily, "we have here on Kratos an Earth-type ecology with one glaring inconsistency—this massive creature which refused to perish when surface conditions became unfavourable. It is a devolved dinosaur with some of the characteristics of a worm, some of the characteristics of an ant, facilities for hibernation and—" he never finished his sentence.

Matthew, manning the screen on the nav deck, reported over the intercom. "Commander, a group of the worm-like creatures, estimated at approximately two hundred and fifty, is rapidly approaching the perimeter. Estimated distance five kilometres. Approach path, north-north-east. Estimated speed, twenty to twenty-five kilometres per hour. Estimated arrival time, thirteen point five minutes plus or minus approximately ten per cent."

"Is it raining out there?" asked Kwango before Conrad could speak.

"Light to moderate," reported Matthew. "Visibility good. Commander, do you have any instructions?"

Conrad's brain got into top gear. "Where are the other robots? Are they outside?"

"No, sir. Mark is carrying out recycling maintenance schedules, Peter is processing animal protein extraction as requested by Miss James, and—"

"Spare me the details. Three exo-skeletons must now be readied for immediate use. Have control systems and power sources checked for optimum efficiency. Execute!"

"Decision noted. Execution proceeds. Estimated time of check-out and make-ready is seven point five minutes. Approaching creatures have different colouration from such creatures already encountered. Approaching creatures are white."

"Bloody marvellous," said Kwango. "It was, of course, to be expected."

"Your next revelations will have to wait," said Conrad. "You, Andreas and Batista are pretty good at using the exo-skeletons. So you can get yourselves harnessed up fast. Batista, how many of those cold nitro-bombs have you got in the fridge?"

"Nine, Commander."

"Then get them out and show Andreas and Kwango

how to arm them. You and the other two have just volunteered to be our first line of defence. You will harness yourselves in the exos, get outside the perimeter and meet our visitors, if you can, one kilometre from the *Santa Maria*. You will toss your nitro-bombs for maximum effect and then take any individual action you see fit. If the bombs don't deflect them, I recommend that you tear up a few trees and beat the bastard's brains out. In the light of Kwango's revelations, try to smash them both ends. While this little party is getting under way, I will take the chopper and a laser rifle and start cutting them up from the sky. Le Gros and James, armed with laser rifles, will stay inside the perimeter for a last ditch defence—if it comes to that. Lieutenant Smith will assume command of the *Santa Maria,* and will oversee operations from the nav deck screen . . . Lieutenant Smith, if the perimeter is breached and the *Santa Maria* is jeopardised, you will instruct Matthew to programme lift-off. You will then follow sub-space return procedure. O.K.?"

"Yes, Commander."

"Let's move, then."

"If it's any consolation, Commander," said Kwango, "they are not coming to attack us."

"They are heading our way."

Kwango shrugged. "Coincidence. We just happen to be in their path."

"I don't buy that kind of coincidence," snarled Andreas. "Come on, black man. Let's go get harnessed up and start tossing cold-nitro around."

Conrad was airborne and over the marauding swarm of deathworms before the men in the exo-skeletons had armed themselves and left the stockade.

He looked down at the dreadful creatures, fascinated. Their means of locomotion was, oddly, by vertical rather than horizontal rippling, and their heads were kept at a fairly constant height of about two metres above ground level. Some, he estimated, were more than a hundred metres long. They would weigh in at considerably more than the three hundred tons estimated by Kwango.

Conrad circled the swarm, then went down to fifty metres altitude, stabilised and put the chopper on automatic, its pace matching the pace of the death worms. He would have liked to go lower; but, as yet, there was no means of knowing how high the creatures could rear. It would be stupid to let himself and the chopper get taken out by an enterprising, if devolved dinosaur.

He reached for his laser rifle. Experimentally, he burned the leading death worm neatly in two. There was a moment or two of convulsion, then both parts began to operate independently. What was even more surprising was that none of the others attacked or attempted to devour their wounded comrade. They simply continued their forward drive as if nothing untoward had happened. Or as if there was a compulsion that superseded their basic programme. So much, thought Conrad, for Kwango's elegant theories.

Then he started burning systematically. Heads and tails. Heads and tails. With both brains gone, the centre section became inert. But still the surviving death worms did not stop to devour the bodies. He had accounted for at least eight death worms by the time the three men in the exo-skeletons arrived on the scene.

Conrad took the chopper up to four hundred metres.

He did not relish the notion of being blown out of the sky by a nitro bomb.

He radioed. "Let them have one, Mr. Andreas, at a range of about five hundred metres. Try to drop it in the middle of the swarm, where they are packed closest together. I want to see what effect it has."

"O.K. Commander. One egg coming up . . . Hey, Kwango, you are the hot-shot boy. Scramble one of yours in the middle of that mess of animated king-size spaghetti."

"To hear is to obey," said Kwango. "Note the style, white man. You may learn something."

"I bet they scatter on the first blast." Conrad identified the voice as Batista's.

"Bet they don't." That was Andreas.

"Next ration of booze?"

"Yeah, Fidel, next ration of booze."

Conrad saw the exo-skeleton in the centre raise its right arm. The throw was beautifully executed. So beautifully executed that, for a moment, it was possible to think of the eight-metre exo-skeleton in which Kwango was harnessed as a living thing in its own right. One of the great legs stretched backwards, seeking and finding secure purchase; then the right arm swung laterally to and fro, reminding Conrad of an Olympic discus thrower limbering up.

Suddenly, the metal arm whipped forward and the nitro bomb soared on its long trajectory.

Kwango had placed his bomb perfectly. The centre of the swarm erupted into a great spout of soil, blood, steam, fragmented death worms. At least ten of the loathsome creatures had been blown to bits. But it did not stop the rest. They did not scatter. They did not attempt to devour what remained of their comrades. They pressed on stoically.

"Howzat!" Kwango's voice.

"Shit and damnation! I have just lost my booze ration." The words, precisely articulated, with only the merest hint of accent, came from Fidel Batista.

Andreas laughed. "Don't worry, sonny boy. We take this lot out and you drink at my expense."

"Mr. Andreas," said Conrad, "deliver three more. Go for the centre again. Try to cut the swarm in half."

Three arms rose in unison. Three more nitro bombs dropped in the centre of the advancing death worms. The swarm exploded grotesquely. Bizarre fragments and gobbits hurled up into the air to rain horribly on the dead, the wounded and the survivors.

Conrad watched, marvelling. The survivors seemed utterly indifferent to the attack. They simply thrashed their way through the mangled remains, gouging great uneven ruts through flesh and soft earth. It was as if they were all possessed by a common purpose, for which they would sacrifice anything. And from the direction in which they were heading, it seemed as if that common purpose was an attack on the *Santa Maria* stockade. Conrad tried to visualise the massed weight of maybe a couple of hundred death worms against the wooden barrier. A lot of the creatures would perish on the sharpened stakes. But some would get through. He knew it.

"Use your remaining bombs at will," he radioed. "Then fall back to the stockade and use laser rifles. They must not be allowed to breach it . . . *Santa Maria*, do you read me?"

"I read you, Commander," answered Lieutenant Smith. "I'm getting it on the screens. Do you think we can stop them?"

"Don't know. Instruct Matthew to look in emergency blast-off programme, set for critical ten from now. We may not be stopping them, but at least we are slowing the bastards down."

The remaining nitro bombs began to explode. More horrendous destruction. The death worms didn't want to know. The survivors, more than a hundred and fifty of them still came on, their vast obscene shapes rippling with fantastic power.

Andreas said: "All bombs away, maestro. We are going back, as per instructions."

Kwango's voice came in. "Not to worry, Commander. They don't want the *Santa Maria*. They don't want us."

"How do you know that, Kwango? Make it fast, and no funnies."

"Because they have small brains. They don't know about space ships, aliens, any damn thing. They operate under a simple bio-programme. I'd stake my life on it."

"You may have to. But suppose their bio-programme, as you call it, tells them they have to pass where we built the stockade?"

Kwango laughed. "If they find they can't go through it, they'll go round it. I hope."

Conrad sighed. "I hope so, too. We don't seem to have made much of a dent in these creatures . . . This bio-programme—have you any idea what it is?"

"Yes, but I don't wish to commit myself just now."

"Kwango, you will bloody commit yourself, or I will

burn you out of that exo-skeleton. This is no time for coyness."

"O.K. Commander. Cool it. I think some kind of migration is in progress."

"Let's hope you are right. Now get back to the stockade and defend it. I'll come down low and burn as many as I can while my laser pile lasts."

"I wish you wouldn't, Commander. We may have critically reduced their number already. I want to find out what they are up to. It has nothing to do with us. Of that, I'm certain."

"You mean, if they bypass the stockade, you want to track them?"

"Exactly that."

"Well, you are the only expert we have. So far, you are jumps ahead of the rest of us. All right, I'll accept your recommendation. Let's all get back and sweat it out."

Kwango, amazingly, was proved right. The death worms did attempt to force the stockade, but not seriously. When half a dozen of them had perished on the sharpened stakes, the rest went round on either side. Conrad ordered the Expendables to hold their laser fire as the monstrous army streamed past. The very ground vibrated with their movements. Even the *Santa Maria* shook.

Conrad stepped out of the chopper and gazed up at the towering star-ship, fascinated. For one dreadful moment, he thought it might shake itself to pieces. Then the crisis was over. The death worms had gone.

"Abort emergency blast-off programme, Lieutenant Smith. Do you read me?"

"I read you. Programme aborted at minus three minutes thirty-seven seconds."

Conrad put the transceiver back in his pocket and turned to Kwango, who had just emerged from the harness of his exo-skeleton.

"So you were right."

"Sorry, Commander. It's a habit I'm not trying too hard to kick."

Conrad grinned. "Kurt, you are one hell of a clown, but you seem to have fluency. Further recommendations?"

"Like I said, we track them."

"Where do you think they are going?"

Kwango shrugged. "Look at the direction. Where else but Mount Conrad, Commander?"

"Why?"

Kwango said solemnly: "The way I see it, we got woman trouble. Let's go find out, shall we? After we have eaten, of course. My! I'm hungry! It must be all this crazy killing."

PHASE THREE

The Rape of the Queen

The sight was no less than utterly astounding. Around the great artificial dome that Kwango had jokingly named Mount Conrad all the migrant death worms had assembled themselves. They looked like monstrous spokes radiating from the hub of a giant wheel, their ninety metres bodies stretched at full length in ruts on the soft ground.

Every five seconds—Conrad had timed it—each death worm lifted its massive head and brought it down with a thud. It was all done in perfect unison, though, as far as could be seen, no signals were given. The precision of the operation, thought Conrad, could not have been bettered by the Brigade of Space Guards.

Matthew had been instructed to leave the hovercar —which Conrad had grounded five hundred metres from the nearest death worm—and take a count of the creatures. He reported that there were one hundred and fifty-seven.

One hundred and fifty-seven three-ton heads hitting dirt simultaneously. No wonder the ground shook.

No wonder fragments of the dome began to fall from its smooth sides.

Besides Matthew, Conrad had brought Lieutenant Smith and Kwango with him in the armoured hovercar. The rest, under the command of Andreas, had been left to see to the security of the stockade and the star-ship.

Conrad glanced at his wristwatch. It had been agreed that contact with the *Santa Maria* would be maintained every fifteen E-minutes. He reached for the hovercar's transceiver.

"Come in, *Santa Maria.* Come in *Santa Maria.* Do you read me? Over."

"Santa Maria to *Groundbug,* I read you loud and clear. Andreas reporting. All well. No activity outside stockade. All systems function. How goes it with you, Boss?"

"We have a box at a super-colossal floor show. We are watching a ring of death worms all pounding their heads rhythmically on the ground at the base of Mount Conrad."

"Any problems, Boss?"

"No problems—yet. And you?"

"No problems. Le Gros and James are taking more samples from the critters that tried to come through instead of round." There was a chuckle. "James has been sick twice, but she has managed to dig out a brain for analysis. That girl has got guts as well as big tits. Le Gros is trying to develop a nasty kind of poison to paralyse the central nervous system of the worms. Two of the robots are cleaning out the filtration system of the recycling unit, and the third is knocking up something special for dinner. They are all on thirty-second stand-to. O.K.?"

"O.K. . . . . Andreas, you haven't programmed for the all-American beefburger again, have you?"

"Sure have, Commander. You'll learn to love it."

"Over and out."

"Over and out."

Conrad stared through the hovercar screen. With each simultaneous thud from one hundred and fifty-seven three-ton heads, the hovercar shook and, more significantly, large chunks of the synthetic hill began to fall away, creating miniature landslides.

"You'd think it was their intention to wreck the joint," said Conrad to no one in particular.

"They are signalling," remarked Kwango confidently. "I think I know what it's all about. It's a battle challenge, and I think I know why."

Conrad glanced at him. Kwango, he thought, was a very brilliant and very irritating man. He got his kicks from springing unpleasant surprises with consummate timing.

"O.K. big genius. You want me to ask why, so I'll ask: Why?"

"Cherchez la femme," retorted Kwango enigmatically. "By the way, Commander, a whole heap of very angry grey death worms are going to put in an appearance pretty damn soon. I don't know what direction they are going to come from, but I would not like it to be right behind us."

Conrad suppressed an impulse to lift Kwango out of his seat with his prosthetic arm and hang one on him. It was only because the black man was being deliberately infuriating that he did not do it.

Instead, Conrad said mildly to the robot: "Matthew, take a laser rifle, station yourself eight hundred metres to our rear, report on any movement of creatures designated as death worms. Maintain radio contact at five minute intervals. Execute."

"Decision noted, Commander. Execution proceeds." Matthew took a rifle and left the hovercar.

Indira spoke. "James, I would like to take a closer look at this ritual. May I do so?"

Conrad was momentarily confused. Things had not been too good between himself and Indira Smith for some time. Yet now she called him James. The hazards of leaving the hovercar and approaching those enigmatic monsters were obvious. Should he slap her down, or let her have her way?

"It's a hell of a risk. What if they register your presence and don't like it?"

Indira touched her thighs. "These tin legs are my insurance. I can do a hundred metres in seven seconds. I could run all day at forty kilometres an hour if I had to. There is no danger."

"That's where you are wrong. On Kratos there is always bloody danger—as long as we have to live with the death worms . . . But, I take your point. You are, as they say, exceptionally endowed. So take a look-see if you want to, but don't get too confident. Kwango and I will cover you with laser rifles. If anything nasty develops, come back at fifty k.p.h. If your route is blocked or if, for any reason, we have to pull out, you make your own way back to the stockade. Agreed?"

"Agreed, James. Thank you."

Indira picked up her laser rifle, got out of the hovercar and cautiously approached the ring of apparently self-hypnotised death worms. They did not register her presence, being wholly absorbed in their ground-shaking ritual. She moved in closer, until she was actually between the end segments of two of the death worms. She inspected the end segments carefully, fighting the feeling of nausea they inspired. The tails were similar to the heads of the monstrous creatures, except that the hideous mouth and eyes were shrunken and almost covered by folds of flesh. Crazily, Indira was reminded of a human penis in cold weather. A super-colossal yet shrunken penis. She cut the thought. It was too disconcerting.

Conrad watched her anxiously from the hovercar.

Kwango said: "Don't let her stay too long, Boss. I got a feeling we're going to get a piece of the action."

Before Conrad could say anything, Matthew reported. "Death worms approaching, Commander. Number visible, zero nine. Estimated distance one point seven kilometres. Estimated speed, twenty-five k.p.h. Do you have instructions?"

"I have instructions. Return to hovercar at maximum speed. Execute."

"Decision noted. Execution pro—" Conrad cut Matthew out and radioed Indira. "Pull back at the double, Lieutenant Smith. We have visitors."

There was no acknowledgment, no response. There, five hundred metres away, plainly visible, Indira was calmly inspecting the end segment of one of the creatures.

Conrad cursed, tried again. Again there was no response. Maybe her transceiver wasn't working. Maybe she had switched the goddamn thing off.

"Shall I go get her?" enquired Kwango.

Conrad shook his head. "I'm not risking two for the price of one." He glanced through the rear window of the hovercar. Matthew was running like the wind. But there was a wave of death worms behind him. They, too, were making good speed. And their numbers had increased. Conrad saw that there were at least thirty, probably more. The bastards must have been popping up out of the ground. Which, of course, was to be expected.

He started the hovercar engine, and looked for an out. There was no out. By the time the hovercar had lifted and started moving it would be outflanked. Matthew tumbled back on board.

"Kill the motor!" said Kwango.

"They may not like the sound of it. If we are quiet, we still have a chance."

Conrad cut the engine. Then he tried to call Indira once more. No response.

But, at least, she seemed to be aware of what was happening. Probably, she had felt the new vibrations in the ground. She turned and saw the advancing wave. She stood still, as if mesmerised.

By the time Matthew had reached the hovercar, the nearest of the creatures was less than two hundred metres behind him. The curved line of approaching death worms now stretched as far as the eye could see. The ground and the hovercar shook violently as the fantastic creatures ploughed over and through the soft ground.

"Run, damn you!" shouted Conrad into the transceiver. "Let's see you do that hundred metres in seven seconds. Smith, that's an order! Run."

But Lieutenant Smith still stood, as if petrified. Conrad swore.

Meanwhile, two of the monstrous things were already passing on either side of the hovercar. They were travelling so fast that the great, moist, rippling bodies were no more than blurs of movement. One of them brushed against the armoured car, tilting it crazily for a second or two. For a terrible moment, Conrad thought the vehicle might turn over; but somehow it righted itself with a teeth-rattling jolt.

Suddenly, the wave was past. The immediate danger to the hovercar and its occupants was receding. Conrad stared through the windscreen. One of the monsters seemed to be heading straight for Lieutenant Smith.

Conrad reached for his laser rifle. "I'm going to get out and start burning," he said. "If the bastards turn, lift off and head back to the stockade as fast as you can."

"Don't," advised Kwango. "Commander, we came to collect vital data. If the ritual is interrupted it may be some time before we get another chance. Indira accepted the risk. This is her party."

Conrad said: "I wish you wouldn't be so bloody right, Kwango, at all the wrong times . . . Do you know any prayers, black man?"

"Boss, I been praying devoutly and silently for the last two minutes."

Both of them peered intently through the windscreen.

The death worm approaching Indira had registered her presence. It was now no more than three metres from her. It raised its massive head to strike out and engulf its prey. But as the head lunged forward, Lieutenant Smith sprang high into the air—a mighty leap of five metres or more. She landed perfectly on the back of the death worm's head. Then she ran along the entire length of its body and leaped off the tail—all this before the creature realised what was happening.

She fell badly, because the tail flicked as she jumped. But she picked herself up and made straight for the hovercar.

As Kwango helped her aboard, Conrad wiped the sweat from his forehead.

"Lieutenant Smith, you are a bloody nut," he said harshly. "Don't ever play such games again."

"I told you I could move rapidly, sir," she said calmly. "Didn't you believe me?"

"Please," said Kwango, gazing intently through the windscreen, "let's not waste time on recriminations. The show is about to begin."

"It had better be good," said Conrad. "The warm-up was, to say the least, interesting."

The white death worms had stopped banging their heads on the ground. They had stopped the motion as the grey death worms came to lie supine alongside them. Now the spokes of the wheel had been doubled —one white, one grey, alternately, in dreadful symmetry.

There was a dull rumbling. Then, from the bottom of the hill, emerged the most monstrous creature so far seen on Kratos. It, too, was clearly a death worm—but it was more than four times the mass of any yet observed.

It cut, ate and thrust its way out of the base of the hill and displayed its vast brilliantly red hulk—two hundred metres long and four metres thick—to the assembled creatures.

There was something revoltingly sensual about its movement. The hideous creature opened its cavernous mouth, flicked out its numerous tongues and tentacles and uttered a high, grunting scream. Then it rolled indolently on its back and displayed an underbelly that exuded a thick milky fluid from an orifice in every single segment.

"Behold the queen!" Kwango's voice was filled with awe.

The queen's behaviour was evidently the signal for a carnage of such frenzy that it would haunt those who witnessed it for the rest of their lives.

Every death worm simultaneously raised its head and answered the cry with roars whose strength was such that the hovercar vibrated with the force. Indira held her hands over her ears; but she could not shut out the dreadful sound.

It lasted perhaps five or six seconds. Then there was a moment of silence, a moment of unreal stillness.

After which, the grey death worms and the white were locked in a battle to the death. They twined themselves round each other like mutually destructive boa-constrictors. They struck like rattle-snakes. They battered each other like charging bulls. They reared and lunged and screamed and killed and died.

Bloody fragments of the creatures were tossed high into the air, to fall messily among the surviving contestants or to make craters of putrescence in the soft ground.

Surprisingly, the carnage was over in a matter of minutes. The white death worms had won the day. Thirty or more of them flung themselves on the seven or eight surviving grey ones and tore them to pieces.

The queen gave her grunting scream once more. It was a signal.

The surviving white death worms approached her. Each reared its frontal segments. From the belly of each, a rod-like section of tissue emerged, as if drawn by magnets.

"They are going to fertilise the queen!" exclaimed Kwango.

"She has more vaginas than they can cope with. I hope the dear lady is not frustrated!"

The queen was not frustrated. The white death worms penetrated her methodically from head to tail, flinging themselves uncaringly across her heaving underbelly so that the tumescent rods slammed down into the waiting orifices with the apparent force of pile drivers. Then they reared up again and repeated the process, their threshing forms at right-angles to the queen and systematically moving along the entire length of her body. At times, three or four of them flung themselves across her side by side, mindlessly and rhythmically going through the monstrous act of copulation.

Each time she was penetrated, the queen's huge body rippled and arched and she gave out a hissing, screaming grunt. Steam rose from her straining body, gouts of milky fluid dripped from her immense length, bubbling from her orifices almost as if, as a result of the frenzy and stimulation, the very liquids in her body had reached boiling point.

Kwango was calmly recording the grotesque sequence with a vid camera. "This has got to be the biggest—and I mean biggest—blue movie in the galaxy," he said drily.

Lieutenant Smith stared through the windscreen, silent, white-faced—like a rabbit confronted by a snake, thought Conrad, glancing at her. He held her hand. It was ice-cold. She didn't even notice that he had touched her.

When the fertilisation process was finished, the surviving males rolled off the queen and lay as though exhausted. The queen's great body continued to arch and pulsate for a while. Her mouth opened and closed spasmodically, the tentacle/tongues flicking out randomly. She seemed to be gasping for air. Presently, she shivered—a shiver that shook the ground—and turned over. Then she began to wriggle indolently among the carnage, gouging and greedily devouring tit-bits from the dead. She ate the flesh of the grey deathworms as well as that of the white. Always, she struck at the back of the head, her tentacle/tongues tearing out great gobbets of flesh and casting them aside so that she could probe deeply for what she wanted.

"She is eating their brains!" said Kwango excitedly. "She is eating their goddamn orange-size brains."

"Now why should she want to do that?" Conrad's voice carried a note of irritation. The whole sequence had sickened him; and, as far as he could judge, Indira Smith was in shock. She hadn't moved. Her hands were still icy cold, and she stared unwaveringly through the windscreen.

"To preserve the bloody genetic programme," said Kwango enigmatically. "Why else? The brain tissue contains the code of behaviour. After this day's work that great cow is going to bring forth god knows how many babies. If they don't operate according to the code, the whole reproduction cycle will fall apart."

"Commander," said Matthew, "the light is failing."

"I know."

"Also, I have to report that some of the surviving

creatures seem to have detected our presence. Have you any instructions?"

Conrad peered through the windscreen. It was true. Three of the death worms had recovered from their exertions. Now that the spell of the fertilisation ritual was broken, they were beginning to take an interest in their environment once more. Sluggishly, they were heading for the hovercar.

"I have, Matthew. Take the controls and get us back to the *Santa Maria*. Execute."

"What the devil is wrong with Lieutenant Smith?" asked Kwango, noting her condition for the first time.

"Kurt, your cleverness is only matched by your stupidity. There is a flash of brandy in the med kit. Get it."

PHASE FOUR

Night Games

Conrad was in his cabin, bringing the log up to date
before he turned in. It had been a very satisfactory and
constructive evening. After dinner—the king-size all-
American beef-burger programmed by Lou Andreas,
but made strangely attractive with piquant sauces and
ample garnishings of the edible fungus and vegetables
of Kratos—there had been a mildly boozy discussion of
the investigation and analysis of the death worms.

Liz James and Chantana Le Gros had each made
useful contributions. James had discovered that the
skin cells were peculiarly vulnerable because of their
very versatility. They were used for breathing, excret-
ing and—in a limited fashion—for ingestion. As a
death worm moved, creating a rut in the ground over
which it traveled, it was able—as she put it succinctly
—to shit, breathe and extract, vital minerals all at the
same time. Le Gros had a further and more interesting
item of information to offer: the death worms could be
destroyed by a liberal application of ordinary salt.
Good old sodium chloride. The death worms could not
cope with it. They had no mechanism for limiting their

ingestion of salt. Therefore, it they had to pass over ground where salt was liberally available, their metabolism would be destroyed.

"So we are in business!" Lou Andreas had exclaimed. "All we have to do now is lift off from this goddamn place, touch down by the nearest piece of sea and set up a salt-extraction plant. Then we come back and create a big perimeter consisting of a salt barrier, and wait while the bastards choke."

"It is not a simple as that, Lou," said Kwango gently. "Our mission is not defensive. It is aggressive. If Kratos is to be colonised, we must take out the death worms by every available means . . . The salt technique is fine, but it does not eliminate it. D.D.T. kills flies, but it does not stop the breeding process. If this planet is going to be colonised by terrestrial man, we have to eliminate the death worms completely."

"And how do you propose to do that?" Conrad had asked.

Kwango smiled. "Simple, Commander. We take out the queens."

And then Kwango had explained his theory—without any humorous digressions, for once. If, as he believed, each hive or nest contained only one functioning queen, it should be possible to set up a migratory chain reaction. According to Kwango, the white death worms that had challenged the occupants of Mount Conrad had lost their own queen. Therefore they needed to find a new one.

So, if several queens could be destroyed—the queens in the million square kilometres already surveyed—an artificial in-balance would be created, resulting in a mass-migration of death worms seeking other queens.

And since the challenge-mating ritual resulted in so much carnage, the death worms would be reducing their own survival potential.

"If we can achieve this effect in the surveyed area," Kwango had concluded, "I submit, Commander, that you would be justified in triggering the colonisation programme. The colonists themselves could use the technique we develop to extend their domain as required." He permitted himself a final Kwangoism. "Thus mankind will have the opportunity to foul up yet another unspoiled planet."

Kwango's reasoning had seemed good. So had the possibilities suggested by the combined work of James and Le Gros. Conrad began to feel mildly optimistic.

The meeting broke up on a rather unusual note. Lou Andreas said: "Commander, I'd like permission to have sex with Miss James." He grinned at her. "The lady is willing."

"I see." Right at the beginning, Conrad had established two basic rules. No Expendable was to take alcohol or any related drug without permission, and no one was to establish a sexual liaison without permission. For obvious reasons.

"Has anyone any objections to Lou's request?" he asked.

Several glances were exchanged, but no one said anything. Kwango stared fixedly at his finger nails. Perhaps, thought Conrad, he was recollecting an unfortunate event in the Pacific Ocean.

"Permission granted," he said. "I hope you have fun . . . You all know the reason why Mr. Andreas and Miss James had to consult me on this matter. We can't afford friction, jealousy, tension—anything that endangers efficiency. I'm sorry our private lives have to be made public, but there it is."

There was a brief silence. Conrad saw Fidel Batista and Chantana Le Gros look at each other in an oddly intimate way. After a moment or two, Chantana gave a barely perceptible nod.

Batista cleared his throat. "Commander, I make the same request for myself and Miss Le Gros."

"O.K. Any objections?" Conrad looked at Kwango and Lieutenant Smith. Kwango was still studying his nails. Indira Smith stared fixedly at the deck.

"Permission granted." He tried to ease the odd tension that had suddenly developed. "Those engaged in—er—joint explorations are entitled to share an extra bottle of wine. The rest of us, I feel, are entitled to a little extra brandy . . . I probably don't have to mention it, but everyone will be available for normal duty tomorrow. In view of what we have recently discussed, I intend to begin to put Kurt's theory to the test. We—or, rather, I—will destroy the first queen. Depending on how that operation goes, we will develop plans for clearing the surveyed area. Good night, ladies and gentlemen."

Now, alone in his cabin, after completing the log and finishing the extra brandy he had allowed himself, Conrad felt curiously empty. He ought to feel sleepy, but he didn't. He wondered why.

There was a knock at the door.

"Come in."

Indira Smith came into the cabin. She was wearing only her short night tunic. She carried a bottle in her hand. It was brandy. It was nearly half empty.

"Permission to report myself, Commander," she said

in a husky voice. "I have stolen and consumed extra booze."

He tried to pass it off lightly. "That's all right, Lieutenant. It's been a rough day. Write yourself a prescription for one half-litre of brandy. No charges will be preferred."

Indira took a swig from the bottle. "I have white hair and tin legs. Am I a woman, or am I not a woman?"

"You are demonstrably a woman."

"Good. Then make love to me." She came towards him. "These breasts have only been handled by about fifty men. Do you fancy being the fifty-first?"

"No."

She gave a shrill laugh. "I am not desirable? The white hair and tin legs bother you?"

"It isn't that. Just that we haven't followed the rules of the house. We haven't asked if there are any objections."

Indira took another swig. "The great Commander has to ask permission of a bunch of exiled psychopaths to lay his second-in-command?"

"Yes. In this matter only, I require permission from the team. Rank does not count in sexual competition. If you were sober, you would know that."

She swayed. "So I'm pissed. You've screwed drunk women before, haven't you?"

He ignored the question. "We keep to the rules. It's important. There isn't going to be one law for us and another law for them."

"Four of your bloody Expendables are too busy to care," she stormed. "So call Kwango and ask for his blessing. Tell him he can have the left-overs."

Conrad sighed. "Why the hell don't you go to bed?"

"I'm going to—with you. Call Mr. Kurt the Magnificent Kwango."

Conrad s'ghed. "If that's the way you want it." He turned to the intercom panel and pressed the button connecting him with Kwango's cabin.

"Kurt, are you there?"

"Yes, suh, Massa Boss. I'se burning de midnight oil over a very interesting computer print-out. Thought you'd be asleep by now. But since you ain't, would you like to know the extrapolated situation if we take out twenty-five queens?"

"Kurt, save that for tomorrow. Just now I have a problem. Have you any objection if—"

Indira slumped. Her eyes rolled upwards and she fell soundlessly to the deck.

"What problem, Massa Boss?"

Conrad passed a hand over her forehead. "Cancel statement. I mean, I'm sorry I disturbed you. It is of no consequence. Sleep well."

"O.K. Massa Boss. Night-night."

"And cut the Uncle Tom crap for good," snapped Conrad angrily. "Or I'll fine you one month's booze ration, and that's a promise."

"Yes, Commander." There was a laugh. "Seems like the Lieutenant turned us both down."

PHASE FIVE

Target: The Queen

It was still raining. Kwango, having run a lot of seem-ingly unrelated data through the computer, had esti-mated that the monsoon—if you could call it that—would last for about a quarter of the Kratos year. But it was nothing like the wet monsoons of Earth. The wind was very light, and the rain was no more than a steady, even drizzle.

Now, as he sat in the hovercar less than a kilometre from Mount Conrad and near one of the vertical shafts that served as a ventilation tunnel to the hive, Conrad felt less than optimistic about his chances of success and survival. But he disciplined himself not to think of anything but the practical problems. He had left de-tailed instructions for the team's future operations in the event of his death. If they were carried out, there was an excellent chance that Kratos could be proved colonisable.

He had with him Batista, James and Matthew. Ba-tista was necessary to arm the cold nitro bombs, and James had asked to come because she wanted to inspect the carnage of the previous day. In particular, she wanted to dig out the brain of a white death worm—if any were left—and take it back for investigation. She wanted to find out if there was any difference—however small—between the brains of the white death worms and the grey.

Matthew was present because Conrad needed his immense strength. The robot would lower him down the ventilation shaft and might have to haul him out in a great hurry.

Batista had constructed six nitro bombs—three for the queen and three for emergencies. He had given them all double trigger mechanisms. Each could be detonated by a timing device or by radio control.

The stench outside the hovercar was overpowering. The wind was fetid with the stink of decaying flesh. Anyone who ventured outside would have to wear a sealed suit and take bottled air.

As Conrad zipped himself up and tested his seals, he gave last minute instructions.

"Fidel, in my absence, you are in command. At your discretion, Liz can investigate the debris, but she must remain in sight at all times. O.K.?"

"O.K. Commander."

"Liz, don't get adventuresome and don't rely on radio contact. That is how we nearly lost Lieutenant Smith."

She gave him a smile and somehow stuck out her breasts not in a provocative way but in a strangely intimate and friendly fashion. Conrad liked Liz. She was so uncomplicated. He hoped she had had a good time with Andreas. She looked as if she had.

"Don't worry about me, James," she said. "I'll be a good girl. But we are going to be worried sick about you."

It was the first time she had called him James. Was it a breach of discipline, he wondered. Ought he to slap her down? Suddenly Conrad smiled at his own idiocy. He was about to be lowered into a hole in the ground with three bloody nitro bombs to blow the guts out of several hundreds tons of devoluted dinosaur. He should worry about discipline?

"Fidel, if I am not back in three hours, assume I'm dead. Blow my three by radio. Even if I don't get as far as the nest, they are bound to do some damage."

"James," said Batista, "you are a stupid man, but you are a good fellow and we have become accustomed to your existence. Please do not terminate it. I will wait five hours if possible before I blow. You may now fine me one booze ration for insubordination."

So now Batista was calling him James. Which meant, very likely, that they thought he was going to get himself killed.

"Two booze rations, Fidel," he said grimly. "One for insubordination and one for anticipated disobedience."

Before he put on the visor of his protective suit, Conrad removed his silver eye-patch and instantly closed both eye lids for ten seconds. During which time he replaced the patch over his good eye. None of the Expendables had ever seen him do this trick. He felt peculiarly naked.

He remembered when the surgeons had offered him the choice. A transplant of one bio-eye or an implantation of one infra-red eye. It had seemed to the surgeons that any ordinary man would have taken a normal human eye. But Conrad was a spaceman. A man who, at times of emergency, had to work in total darkness. What would he not have given for an infra-red eye that time when, as a junior lieutenant, he was doing hull inspection on the old *Lavoisier* and all his suit circuitry failed and his support pack folded when he fell against the antenna. Three minutes of air left, and he had to feel his way back to the lock. With an infra-red eye he could have seen that it was only ten or twelve steps away. But he had spun in the darkness on the end of his line before his magnetic shoes made contact, and he had lost all sense of direction. He never did make it back to the air-lock. He died.

But the bright boyo on the minitor was a fast mover. The moment he stopped getting signals from life-support, he hit the panic button. And the emergency squad broke records going through the lock to pull in Conrad before death was irreversible.

So Conrad took some pride and pleasure from the fact that he now possessed an infra-red eye. He would never be lost in the darkness again.

He opened his eye and adjusted to a world that was, illusorily, red, black, blue, white in the oddest places. James and Batista looked like bizarre colour picture negatives, Matthew was black. And everything glowed far too brightly. Conrad gasped, and blinked once or twice. Then he was O.K. He glanced at James, and grinned. Her eyes, mouth, breasts, crotch were all brighter than the rest of her. Evidently, the night with Andreas had been successful. He thought of making some sly comment, but wisely decided against it.

"Give me the nitro bombs, Fidel." They were black, being very cold, despite the vacuum cladding. Conrad hooked them on to his belt. Then he turned to Matthew. "How much nylon cord have you got?"

"Four hundred metres, Commander. I also have a reserve coil of two hundred metres, breaking strength two, five, zero kilos."

"That should be more than enough. Let's go."

"Good luck, James," said Batista. "I'll borrow from someone else to drink your health tonight."

"Try not to be a bloody hero," said Liz.

The shaft was open, unlike some that had been discovered. No doubt Kwango would eventually offer some perfectly logical explanation why some were sealed and some were not. Maybe it had to do with the change of seasons.

Conrad let out a sigh of relief when Matthew began to lower him into the dark. With infra-red vision, the surface world was too bright, too disturbing, too full of heat.

The coolness of the shaft was pleasant. Matthew had been instructed to lower him at the rate of ten metres a minute. The strata through which the shaft passed had subtly different and interesting glows. It was, thought Conrad, like being lowered through a hole in a layer cake.

When he hit the bottom, Matthew radioed: "Descent time four point two nine minutes. Depth: four two point nine metres. Do you read me, Commander? Do you have instructions?"

"I read you. Instructions as follows: One: remain ready to retrieve from three hours from now. Two: If retrieval not accomplished within time limit, return to hovercar. Three: report to Mr. Batista that my instructions are that he return to base. Four: if Mr. Batista objects, neutralise him with minimum force and proceed as instructed. If Miss James objects, neutralise her with minimum force and proceed as instructed. Execute."

"Instructions received. Execution proceeds."

Conrad unhooked the nylon cord. Having assured himself that the three nitro bombs were O.K., he entered the tunnel that led to the hive.

It was a long, uphill walk. He had plenty of time to wonder what he would do if he encountered a death worm coming out of the hive. There would only be one thing to do. He couldn't retreat fast enough. He would just have to go with a bang.

He soon discovered that his hypersensitive infra-red vision wasn't the total answer to darkness. He could "see" the walls of the tunnel but as through a thick blue-black fog. Twice he almost fell into small cavities he hadn't seen. He was thankful that the cold nitro was stable. The old conventional nitro-glycerine would have blown him to glory.

He knew that he was near the hive when he felt and heard the strange regular throbbing he had experienced on first discovering Mount Conrad. Soon, perhaps, he would find out what it was.

His environment evaluation unit, a small pack clipped on his right forearm, told him that temperature and humidity were rising, that air pressure was falling, that he was approaching ground level and that there was slight but insignificant radio-activity. His electrochron told him that more than forty-five minutes had elapsed since project commencement. Clearly, he wasn't going to have too much time for exploring the hive, allowing for the return journey.

Suddenly, the tunnel debouched into a huge chamber, in the centre of which was a great, flat-topped mound, round which a spiralling track ran. Conrad stood still for several minutes, peering through the misty gloom, his brain consciously and laboriously translating the faint infra-red radiation into a coherent picture.

The ground shook beneath his feet. It shook because lying around the vast chamber were the male death worms, apparently dormant or sleeping. Now he knew what the throbbing was caused by. It was caused by a faint unified rippling of those immense bodies, which resulted in their heads being lifted perhaps half a metre from the ground and then slamming down. Perhaps the action was connected with respiration or some necessary muscular activity.

He wished very much that it had been possible for him to use normal vision and a lamp. It was very hard translating the faint patterns of infra-red radiation into a meaningful image. But all the evidence so far indicated that these dreadful creatures were extremely light sensitive. So he would just have to do the best he could.

Presently, he was able to construct a fairly clear picture in his mind. The sleeping male death worms were ranged—almost protectively—around the great central mound. Their vast, pulsating, horrific bodies glowed dully in the foggy darkness. There was no sign of the monstrous queen. Maybe she lay on top of the miniature mountain that dominated the interior of the nest. It seemed a reasonable supposition. The surviving males were doubtless protecting her during gestation.

The miniature table mountain in the centre of the nest seemed to be above five hundred metres high. The prospect of climbing it was daunting. But it looked as if it would have to be done.

Later, Conrad would have time to marvel at the mindless engineering talent that enabled the death worms to construct a nest that was one kilometre high, provide an efficient ventilation system and construct a redoubt where the queen would be safe.

But, for the time being, he had to concentrate on his mission of destruction. He glanced at his electrochron. Forty-eight minutes had already elapsed. There was no time to waste.

He had already noticed that tunnels abounded at the base of the hive. He could only "see" about a hundred and fifty metres to right or left. But he registered eighteen circular blacknesses spread at regular intervals and deduced that tunnels existed all round the perimeter.

The big problem was: when he left his own tunnel, how would he find it again? Fortunately, the problem had been anticipated—not by Conrad but by Kurt Kwango. And it had been solved by Lou Andreas.

Andreas, engineering genius that he was, had constructed ten hot "marbles" which now lay in Conrad's thigh pocket. The marbles, powered by tiny mercury batteries, would radiate black heat for six hours. For Conrad with his infra-red vision, they would glow like ancient aircraft landing-lights on a runway.

He took one out and pressed it experimentally into the wall on the right hand side of his tunnel. It shone like a beacon. He pressed another one on the left hand side. Now he would know where to aim for, how to get the hell out, if he was lucky enough to be able to plant his nitro bombs under the queen.

Eight "marbles" left. Every twenty-five paces, as he

threaded his way cautiously towards the huge, slumbering mass of death worms round the central mound, he dropped one of the marbles, glancing back to check that his line of approach remained straight.

As he came near to the creatures, he was glad once more that he was on infra-red vision. He could see nothing in detail, only the heat shimmer radiated from the pulsating, supine monsters. But in imagination he could see—he clamped down on that. To hell with imagination. With iron self-discipline he temporarily abolished it. Otherwise, he would have thrown up, passed out or run for his life. There would be time for nightmares later. If he lived . . .

The next problem was: how to pass the creatures and scale the mound on top of which, he was certain, the queen lay in gestation? Sweat began to form on his forehead. There was no way round. He would have to climb over them. Even with his prosthetic arm, it would be difficult, if not impossible, to toss the nitro bombs on top of the small mountain. And even if he succeeded, how could he be absolutely sure that the queen was there and that she would be destroyed? Quite possibly, she might be nestling in a chamber inside the mound.

He would simply have to go and find out. And fast. The electrochron told him that sixty-nine minutes had now elapsed.

He summarised the relevant facts in his mind. Small brains, rudimentary nervous system, low skin sensitivity. If he could climb over the bastards it would surely provide no more irritation than a mouse crawling over a sleeping anaconda.

Would the anaconda wake? Now was the time to find out.

There were three death worms between him and the gouged out spiral track at the base of the mound. No doubt that track was the route by which the queen descended when she was ready to come out and play.

Biting his tongue to distract him from thinking about the consequences, Conrad put out his prosthetic arm, reached high and took a grip on the thick soft skin of the nearest death worm. His timing was bad. The creature's body rippled as he grasped. He was lifted clear of the ground, then flung down. He lost his grip and his balance, falling heavily. The breath was knocked out of him. Rivulets of sweat trickled down his face. He put his hand on one of the cold nitro-bombs. Any moment, he expected to see a fearsome, glowing head strike at him. Well, he would at least take a few of the bastards with him.

But nothing happened. Conrad got to his feet shakily. He tried again, waiting till another ripple had passed the segment he was hoping to climb. He took a firm grip once more and hauled himself up the creature's side, using his bio-arm to hold him while the prosthetic arm reached higher. He had hauled himself up on to the death worm's back before the next ripple came. He immediately lay down and hung on for dear life.

When the ripple had passed, he stood up and tried to decide if he could jump on to the back of the next one. The gap was at least four metres. He knew he wasn't going to make it. If he fell and hurt himself or disturbed the bloody things, that would be the end of the operation. There was two more death worms between him and the base of the mound. He wished, uselessly, that he had Indira's thin legs. She would have cleared the three bodies in one magnificent leap.

But he didn't have tin legs. So he had to climb laboriously down and up, down and up, and down, timing his movement to avoid the steady rippling.

He was amazed to find that he had reached the base of the mound without rousing the creatures whose bodies he had crawled over.

Now all he had to do was march up the spiral track. Seventy-four minutes had elapsed. Therefore, assuming his return journey would take the same time, he had sixteen minutes to get up there, plant the bombs and start back.

Puffing, aching and with his heart pounding painfully, he reached the top of the mound—having made himself walk twenty paces then run twenty paces—in eleven minutes. The top was not flat as he had supposed. It was concave. Just like a shallow nest.

And there in the nest was the immense, fantastic coil of the queen's body. It glowed. It throbbed. All two hundred metres of it exuded heat and intimations of developing life. Each segment of that opulent body contained a womb wherein a new death worm waited to be born.

Conrad recalled the fertilisation procedure and was again moved to wonder. For a precious three minutes he stood on the edge of the nest, marvelling at the fecundity of nature. Then he shook himself out of his semi-trance and scrambled down the gently sloping side of the nest. The slumbering queen ignored his presence with regal indifference.

He armed the first nitro bomb, setting it for detonation at one hundred minutes from arming, and placed it under her head. He nerved himself to lift folds of flesh with his prosthetic arm so that he could be sure the bomb was centrally placed. The second one he pushed under her centre segments. The last one he placed under the tail/second head.

The lady did not notice. He was immensely grateful. He scrambled back up the side of the nest.

He glanced at his electrochron. One hundred and nineteen minutes had now elapsed. He was in trouble.

He made good time getting down the spiral track, though he stumbled twice and, on the second occasion, did some damage to his ankle. Now he was limping. That was bad.

Again he had trouble climbing over the quiescent death worms. He lost his balance when he was on the back of the middle one and fell down its slippery side. He did more damage to his ankle, and had to bite his tongue so that he would not cry out with the pain.

He had fallen in a bad place. At that point, the body of the middle death worm was less than half a metre from the outside one. He was jammed between them. Each time the ripples passed through the parallel segments, he was lifted clear of the ground and slammed back. Yet more damage to the unfortunate ankle.

Somehow, he managed to ease his prosthetic arm free, reach up the side of the last one, dig his metal fingers into its flesh and haul himself up. Crazily, he didn't seem to care any more if he disturbed the creature. The pain in his ankle was agonising. What the hell! If the bastard woke up, it didn't bloody matter. The queen would be blown. Mission accomplished. No doubt Lieutenant Smith would analyse the debris; and

Kwango would sift the evicence and conclude that it was no longer necessary to do it the hard way.

He fell off the back of the third death worm and hurt himself some more. This time, it was his arm.

"Jesus," he thought. "I've made a real bloody mess of this little exercise." Through mists of pain he saw that one hundred and thirty eight minutes had elapsed.

He turned from the glowing and pulsating death worms and looked for his flare path in the apparently infinite blackness of the huge chamber. For a while he couldn't find it. Evidently he had come back over the death worms at a different place. Cautiously he limped ten paces to the right, peering out into the darkness. Still no hot marbles. He gave himself the horrors briefly by thinking that he might have to spend what was left of the hundred minute fuse trying to find his exit tunnel. Then he pulled himself together and limped twenty paces to the left. And found it.

Eight bright shiners, leading in an almost straight line to the ones that shone on each side of the tunnel. He looked once more at his electrochron. One hundred and forty seven minutes elapsed. Twenty-three minutes to get back down the bloody tunnel to the shaft. He had taken much longer than that to get from the shaft to the chamber. He wasn't going to make it.

But he did make it.

He was nineteen minutes late, and he had passed out twice in the tunnel because of the pain in his ankle.

And he survived only because Matthew was a very logical robot.

When Matthew had hauled him to the surface, he stayed conscious long enough to register—even with the limitation of infra-red vision—that the armoured hovercar was a wreck, having been half smashed into the ground, and that there was no sign of James or Batista. But he did see the burnt and fragmented remains of a death worm.

"What happened?" he demanded thickly.

"Sequence of events is as follows," began Matthew.

But Conrad had used up all his energy, all his courage, all his staying power. He gave a great sigh, his knees became rubber, and he passed out once more. And stayed out.

Matthew surveyed his inert form, checked pulse, breathing and temperature. Then, very gently, he lifted Conrad up, cradled the limp body in his arms and began to march back to Base One.

Presently, the ground shook with a great triple explosion. Matthew swivelled his vision system and looked behind him. Mount Conrad had disappeared. Where it had stood, a mushroom shaped cloud of dust and debris rose.

The robot observed the phenomenon for a few moments, having decided that the event had significance. But Conrad, mercifully, remained uninterested.

Presently, Matthew renewed his march. He left a thin trail of blood all the way back to Base One. It dripped from where splintered bone stuck through the flesh of Conrad's leg.

PHASE SIX

Consolidation

The first thing Conrad saw when he opened his eyes was the face of Lieutenant Smith. He thought she looked entirely beautiful—white hair and· all. He had been having nightmares. Bad ones. His body was dripping with sweat. He had dreamed he was back in that dreadful chamber, that the hot marbles had disappeared, that he had roused one of the death worms when he climbed over it, that the nitro bombs were ticking thunderously like surrealist clocks . . .

He looked gratefully at the calm face and the silvery hair. It was soft, lovely hair . . . Suddenly, he realised he was getting normal colour register. Someone had put the patch back over his infra-red eye. Strangely, he felt embarrassed.

Then he remembered.

He tried to sit up. But there was one hell of a pain in his leg. He sank back on the pillow.

"What happened?" he demanded. "James and Batista—*what happened?*"

"Welcome back," said Lieutenant Smith softly. "You

are a hard man, Commander. You broke three bones, and theoretically you should not have been able to walk down that tunnel. Then you get a massive infection from some local bug. And after that you got pneumonia and hit forty degrees Centigrade. You ought to be dead. Maybe you are superhuman, or maybe I'm a bloody good doctor. Take your pick."

"What happened, Lieutenant?" He tried to get an edge of authority into his voice, but it sounded plaintive—just like the voice of an old man.

Indira sighed. "I knew you would be a terrible patient. Can't you ever relax?"

This time he managed to sit up, despite the excruciating throbbing the action produced in his leg. *"What bloody happened?"* he shouted. "Lieutenant, you are going to tell me. That is an order." He began to cough, and that made the pain worse, and that made him sweat more.

"Lie down, then, and I'll tell you." She fluffed up his pillow and lowered him down to it. "The bad news first. Liz is dead, Fidel is only half-dead. I have him in intensive care. I think he'll pull through."

"How did it happen?"

"First some more bad news. I have assumed temporary command, James. I will not relinquish command until, in my professional opinion, you are able to take up active duty and make sound decisions. I have entered this in the log, and the entry is countersigned by the rest. Message ends."

Conrad gazed at her, a mixture of emotions surging through him—relief, resentment, gratitude and sheer anger. He wasn't strong enough to cope with all that.

He just lay there, confused, exhausted—wishing, at the same time, that he could kiss her and shake her till her teeth rattled.

"My mind is now clear," he said feebly. "Thank you for coping, but I am now able to resume command."

"You are not," she retorted cheerfully, "and if you try to get tough or exhaust yourself with anger, I'll stick a needle in your arm and put you to sleep. You will rest and recuperate. That is an order. Understood, Commander?"

He opened his mouth to bellow at her. But the sound would not come. He took a couple of deep breaths, and then let out a great sigh. "Understood—Commander . . . Now, goddammit, tell me what happened."

"Matthew has put it all on record, in great detail, in his own impeccable style. But as you are not yet ready for a thousand words of robotesse, I'll just give you the precis. Liz found a hole—not a vertical shaft. It went down at an angle of about forty-five degrees. She had her laser rifle with her, and the hole did not look as if it had been used recently. There was, apparently, some vegetation growing over the entrance. So she made the tragic mistake of shining her torch down in to see if there was anything of interest.

"Alas, there was. A death worm was already in the tunnel. The light instantly activated it. You can guess the rest. It came out fast. For reasons that will never be known, Liz couldn't stop it with the laser. Fidel, who was in the hovercar, had her in view all the time. When he saw her running for dear life, he armed a nitro bomb and rushed out towards her.

"Matthew, standing vigil by your shaft, registered the entire disaster. He didn't do anything because his priority instruction was to wait for your return for three hours. Fidel didn't have time to programme him.

"The death worm rapidly overtook Liz and those dreadful tongues shot out of its mouth and wrapped round her. Fidel, for some reason, hadn't taken his laser rifle—it all happened so quickly—and all he had was the nitro bomb. The sight of Liz being drawn into that cavernous mouth must have unhinged him. He got the timing wrong and the range wrong. The bomb fell short and detonated too quickly . . . Liz couldn't have suffered much . . . It blew her and the death worm. But it also blew an arm off Fidel and ripped his stomach open. He was just plain lucky that veins and arteries were cauterised in the blast. The death worm lived long enough to wreck the hovercar. So Matthew reasoned that, since his secondary responsibilities had been eliminated, he could wait longer for you . . . He is one hell of a good robot."

Conrad was silent for a few moments, taking it all in. "How did you retrieve Fidel?"

"Kurt took an exo-skeleton and got there as fast as he could. He picked up what was left of Fidel and broke the land speed record for exos getting back. Then he went back again and inspected the debris . . . The entire hill had crumbled, James. You got the queen—Kurt scooped out bits of her—but a few males survived. Kurt gave all he could find the Kwango treatment."

"What the hell is the Kwango treatment?"

Indira Smith gave a faint smile. "I think you have to be a crazy black genius to operate it. You know how good he is with an exo . . . Well, the way Kurt tells it, it was simply a matter of stamping on the forebrain.

Then, while the thing is registering that little surprise, you skip down the length of the body and stamp on the rear brain. He claims he took out seven survivors."

Conrad began to laugh, a trifle hysterically. He had a sudden vivid image of Kwango's graceful dance of death in the exo-skeleton. The laughter turned into coughing, and the coughing hurt.

"I can believe it," he managed to say at last. "It has the ring of the authentic Kwango, whom we have all learned to love and hate."

"There's a bit more good news. Kurt and Lou have already destroyed the rest of the hives in the block of one million square kilometres already surveyed. The queens are dead, and almost most of the males."

"How the hell did they manage to do that?"

"When you blew the queen, you also blew the hive. Kurt examined the debris and was able to deduce what a cross-section would be like. Also, more important, where the weak points are. He and Lou worked out that if they drilled through the dome itself—which is surprisingly thin, they could drop three bombs in the nest, more or less where you placed them. When the nest itself blows, the fragments and pressure waves hit the wall of the hive just in the right place. Then the dome collapses and brings the rest down with it."

Conrad said unsteadily: "I have been out a long time, apparently. How long?"

"Eleven days. Your heart stopped twice, and your lungs were so full of fluid that you ought to have died permanently. You're a very obstinate man."

"I also have a very obstinate doctor . . . How long are you going to keep me in this bloody bed?"

Indira gazed at him critically, then ran her hands

through her soft white hair. Conrad thought she looked very tired, but had the wit not to say so. Now, he told himself with grim satisfaction, she is finding out what it feels like to be in command, to have to make all the important decisions.

She took his temperature, then listened to his heart. Finally, she told him to cough while she ran the stethoscope over the key points of his chest and back.

"Your left lung is clear, but I'm still not too happy about the other one . . . The heart is O.K. though. That's something."

"How long?"

She shrugged. "Nine days, perhaps, if you behave yourself. Twice that if you don't. Message received?"

Conrad let out an exasperated sigh. "Received and understood—Commander."

"Good. If you attempt to leave this bed without permission, you will forfeit one booze ration, and I shall make an entry in the log—duly countersigned—that in my professional opinion you are unfit to resume command of this expedition. And how do you like that?"

Conrad grinned. "You are learning fast."

Indira turned to go. "Kurt sends you a message. He asked me to tell you that he still thinks you are the best living kamikaze pilot in the business. Do you wish to send a reply?"

"Tell him: king's pawn to K.4."

By the time Conrad was pronounced fit to resume duty, the rainy season was at its height; but this did not prevent a lot of useful work being done. The survey of the million kilometre block that had been cleared of death worm hives was now repeated in detail so that large

scale maps could be prepared for the benefit of possible
colonists. With the help of two of the robots, Andreas
had begun systematic seismic surveys of areas which,
according to Kwango, would be most likely to contain
oil or coal deposits. Some of the results—especially to
the north—seemed promising. But it would be impossible to tell whether oil or coal existed in useful quanti-
ties without actually drilling. And the *Santa Maria* was
not equipped for drilling on that scale.

While all this was going on, Kwango continued his
study of the habits of the death worms. With instruction from Andreas, he had rapidly become a proficient
chopper pilot. When the hives had been destroyed not
all of the males had died. The survivors had migrated.
The strange thing was that they seemed to know where
to go. They did not waste time heading for hives that
had already been demolished. Kwango tracked some of
the migrations from the air. The fantastic creatures
seemed to realise that it was no good heading for the
cleared area. The survivors migrated east and west, but
not north or south. Presumably, they were restricted to
a fairly narrow temperature zone. Kwango was also
lucky enough to witness their hunting techniques.
When the death worms came across the large herds of
the deer-like creatures that abounded on Kratos, the
migrating swarm would automatically separate into
hunters and trappers. The trappers would make a great
detour round the herd then form themselves into a vast
semi-circle, head to tail. The hunters positioned themselves immediately behind the herd, threshing about
and making a great deal of noise. The terrified creatures would then be stampeded into the waiting semi-

circles. The hunters would follow and the circle would be closed. Then the slaughter would begin.

Meanwhile, Lieutenant Smith and Chantana Le Gros carried out systematic research on the many specimens of flora and fauna that were brought to them. Big game had now returned to the vicinity of Base One. Conrad showed the robots how to set net traps and doped lures, and how and where to make concealed pits. The largest creature they caught approximated to a Terran giraffe. It, too, was a ruminant. It yielded succulent meat that could not be rivalled by the best beef animals of Earth.

Batista made a good recovery. He could not hope to be fitted with a prosthetic limb until—and if—he returned to Earth. But he had adapted skilfully, and was now known with some affection as the one-armed bandit.

Conrad sent an interim to report to Terra by subspace radio. It was necessarily brief. The energy drain for sub-space transmission was huge. The generators on the *Santa Maria* could only supply the necessary juice for a matter of seconds. Otherwise they would burn out.

The message read: "Kratos colonisation prospects excellent. Make ready first hundred colonists for m/t approx three E-months from receipt of message. Message ends. Signal receipt. Conrad."

That evening, after a mildly celebratory dinner consisting entirely of food derived from Kratos, Conrad, in the course of a discussion with Batista about a limited mining operating to obtain minerals that could be used to make good the depleted stock of explosives, caught

Indira Smith's eye. They exchanged brief but subtly communicative glances. Suddenly, Conrad forgot what he was talking about. He only knew that silently he had asked a question, and silently had received an answer.

Batista was momentarily puzzled. Then he looked at Conrad and at Indira, and understood.

Conrad stood up, feeling a fool. "I made the rules of the game, and I have to abide by them. I wish to spend the night with Lieutenant Smith. Does anyone have any objections?"

Chantana smiled, shaking her head. Andreas said lightly: "Brandy for the non-combatants, Boss?"

Conrad smiled faintly. "That, too, seems to be a rule of the house."

Kwango went to Indira and kissed her. "Some other time, Lieutenant?"

She held his hand. "Yes, Kurt. Some other time."

Kwango sighed. Then he dipped his finger in a glass of wine and touched her forehead. "This is one hell of a woman. She brought me back from the dead and she ran the goddamn show while the good Commander was having an attack of the vapours. I give you a toast, friends. May God bless all who sail in her."

And suddenly, there was much laughter.

It was a good night, one that both of them would long remember. For Indira, many ghosts were exorcised. Conrad was amazed at the passion and pleasure they gave each other, amazed also to discover an exhilarating kind of peace he had never previously known.

He dreaded the morning, thinking that it would bring complications. It didn't. Indira, the sex-goddess of the night, simply became Lieutenant Smith once more. An Expendable, ready for hazardous duty . . .

Confirmation of the receipt of Conrad's message came forty-six K-days after transmission. Which wasn't bad, considering sub-space lag of fifty days plus had been anticipated.

It read: "Acknowledged. First hundred in S.A. ready for transmission. Signal when you are ready to receive."

Conrad assembled his team. "We are going to build a town," he said, "two kilometres south of Base One. We are going to build a town that will eventually accommodate two thousand people. The river runs close to the site, and we will also sink wells at appropriate places. The advance contingent will consist of one hundred Terrans. At first, they will live in log cabins, as their ancestors did when opening up new territories. We will design the town, build the cabins, construct a hospital and a school. We will provide everything they can possibly need."

"A town has to have a name," said Andreas. "How about Conradsville?"

"Thank you, Lou, but no. Unless anyone objects, it will be called Jamestown, in memory of Liz. Someday, I hope, someone will put up a statue of Elizabeth James in the main square. In fact we will require it. And the inscription will read: Elizabeth James, Expendable, who died proving Kratos."

"If he doesn't get the breasts right," said Andreas with feeling, "I'll come back to this place and stamp all over him. Liz was a great woman. She had magnificent breasts."

Influx

SEQUENCE ONE

Panorama

Day 107. The *Santa Maria* lifted from Base One for low level orbital survey prior to establishing Base Two, for exploration purposes only, in the temperate zone of Continent A. On board were Conrad, Kwango and Matthew. Lieutenant Smith remained in command at Base One. With Andreas, Batista, Le Gros and the three robots, she began the construction of Jamestown, designed to provide accommodation for two thousand people. Lieutenant Smith herself had become very proficient in the use of an exo-skeleton. Presently, log cabins would rise; roads would be marked out, levelled and surfaced with crushed rocks; wells would be sunk; drainage systems dug.

Day 119. The *Santa Maria* touched down in an area where magnetometric survey indicated rich mineral deposits. The nearest death worm hive was nine hundred kilometres to the south.

Day 132. Matthew discovered a mountain consisting almost entirely of rich iron ore. Conrad recorded the discovery on the map, designating it as Matthew's Find. He thought it was probably the first time anything had ever been named after a robot.

Day 147. Entry in Commander's log, Base One: This day, one exo-skeleton wrecked and Lou Andreas, operating it, badly injured by landslide while quarrying stone for the roads of Jamestown. Injuries include broken leg (clean break, no problem), crushed ribs (one penetrating left lung), and fractured skull with possible brain damage. Have set leg and am preparing to operate on chest, Le Gros assisting. Patient did not return to consciousness after accident. Impossible yet to determine extent of cerebral injuries. Have informed Commander, *Santa Maria,* of situation. Construction work continues, Batista supervising. (Signed) Indira Smith, temporary commander, Base One.

Day 147. Entry in Commander's log, Base Two: Substantial bauxite deposits discovered fifteen kilometres south west of Base Two. Aluminum as well as iron will now be available in quantity to colonists. Received from Base One concerning extensive injuries suffered by Andreas while quarrying in exo-skeleton. If injuries result in incapacitation, Base One's construction schedule will be badly hit. In which case, Base Two operations will have to be modified. Have signalled commander Base One to keep me informed. Meanwhile, Base Two survey projects proceed as planned. (Signed) James Conrad, commander, *Santa Maria.*

Day 151. Signal from Base One to Base Two: Andreas will live, but brain damage extensive. I am not competent to deal with it. Patient requires attention best neurosurgeons of Terra. Await your instructions, Smith.

Day 151. Signal from Base Two to Base One: Received your message on return from chopper survey of inland lakes system. Sorry about Lou. Keep him going till we can put him in S.A. Am curtailing Base Two operation. Expect to return in five or six days. Conrad.

Day 157. The *Santa Maria* touched down at Base One precisely on its first touch down point, James Conrad navigating. Andreas was lying on a bed in the pre-fab hospital room that had been erected near the Expendables' living hut before the star-ship left. There was no sign of Lieutenant Smith or the others. He guessed she would be exo-working at Jamestown. He guessed right. He called her and learned that she was already on her way back. Conrad had not had time to do anything more than glance at Jamestown on the screens. Progress was better than he had expected. Later he learned why. The one-armed bandit was using an exo with remarkable skill.

Lieutenant Smith laid her exo down and unharnessed. Then she joined Conrad, who had been gazing at Andreas for several minutes.

Andreas seemed comfortable. His head was bandaged, and he lay on his back with his eyes open, expressionless. Conrad had tried talking to him, but got no response. He just stared up at nothing.

Conrad turned to Lieuttnant Smith. "You have had a rough time, Indira. But I see you got a lot of work done."

"Lou has had a rough time, James . . . I did the best I could." Her voice wavered. "But, dammit, I am no brain surgeon."

He held her gently, gently kissed her. "You can't be everything. You are one hell of a good heart surgeon. The infallible Kwango says so. And you are a five-star Expendable. I say so. Isn't that enough?"

Suddenly, she was crying. "No, it's not enough! I—I feel as if Lou were my brother. I feel as if I failed him."

"Lou is *our* brother," corrected Conrad gently. "Fidel is our brother also, and Liz was our sister. We are an élite corps. We belong to each other . . ." He turned towards Andreas. "Hey, Lou! You think Lieutenant Smith is no good?"

No response. Lou Andreas gazed tranquilly at nothing.

"Lou wants me to speak for him," said Conrad. "He wants me to say: thank you for trying so goddamn hard. He says he's sorry for lousing up the schedule, and he asks me to remind you that he made you learn to love the all-American beefburger—Kratos style."

"Tell him," sobbed Indira, "tell him I did my best."

"He already knows . . . Now let's get him into the *Santa Maria* and under S.A. If you can't face the cooling procedure, Matthew can do it. He's fully programmed."

Suddenly, she pulled herself together. "Andreas is my patient, Commander. I will put him down."

"O.K., Lieutenant. Proceed . . . When we get back, Lou will have the best brain surgeons in the solar system. This, I swear."

Day 179. Entry in Commander's log, *Santa Maria*. This day, the first stage in the construction of Jamestown is completed. We now have the necessary facilities to support the first colonists. Have signalled Terra to this effect.

Day 205. In the evening, Conrad held a party in the saloon of the *Santa Maria*. He thought he was the only one who knew why. He was wrong. Kwango knew why.

The menu was special. The foods were the foods of Kratos, but the wines were the wines of Earth. It seemed symbolic.

After everyone had eatern and drunk just a little too much, Conrad decided it was time to make a speech.

"Ladies and gents," he began clumsily.

"Cancel statement," interrupted Kwango. "There are no ladies and gents present, Massa Boss, only damn awful Expendables."

"Well, then, damn awful Expendables," amended Conrad, "when I first met you, I thought you were a horrible bunch of misfits. After spending much time in your company, I see no reason to change my opinion. But you have proved Kratos. And I am proud to have known you. I speak like this only because I am slightly pissed and because this evening has a special significance. It is—"

"New Year's Eve," said Kwango.

Conrad gazed at him severely. "Black scum!" he said without heat.

"White trash," retorted Kwango.

"Why the hell do you always have to anticipate?"

"Isn't that what you hired me for, Massa Boss?"

Conrad sighed. "I suppose so. But it gets wearing.

And, incidentally, for insubordination you will now be fined—"

"One booze ration!" The four voices were perfectly in unison.

"Happy New Year, everybody," said Conrad. "We have survived on Kratos one planetary cycle. Tomorrow, Matthew and his merry band will erect the matter receiver in Jamestown. Don't ask me how it works. That information is stored only in Matthew's circuits and the *Santa Maria* computer's memory banks. But, pretty soon, now, the covered wagons are going to roll across the prairie."

Fidel Batista stood up. "James—yes, I know, that is going to cost me a booze ration—James, may I propose a toast?"

"Fidel, you may."

"It is an English toast," said Fidel. "Peculiarly English. They are a mad people, as we all know. But, in some things, they have style."

"Heah, heah," said Kwango in an atrocious imitation of the ancient Oxford accent.

"To absent friends," said Fidel, raising his glass.

"To absent friends," responded Conrad, raising his own glass. He thought of Liz and Lou, and was glad that only one eye could become moist.

SEQUENCE TWO

Mission Ends

It was a fine, spring-like afternoon. Conrad sniffed the air appreciatively and glanced about him at Jamestown. The sunlight gave it a slightly romantic aspect—rather like one of the deserted ghost towns in those quaint twentieth century westerns. But, presently, it would look less like a ghost town and more like a boom town. For the first hundred colonists were on their way.

Matthew, at Conrad's request, had tried to explain to him the theory of matter transmission by sub-space. But Conrad was little wiser. He had also looked up sub-spatial m/t in the *Santa Maria*'s tape library. He got a lot of maths for his pains and very little enlightenment. Even the hitherto omniscient Kwango could not master the theory—which afforded Conrad some small satisfaction.

The matter receiver had been erected in Andreas Square, near to the large insulated storage chamber where the sealed cylinders would be kept until their occupants could be taken out of S.A.

Conrad idly imagined a string of one hundred steel sausages, somewhere between Kratos and Terra, sixteen light years away. He imagined them hurtling through space at unimaginable velocities, annihilating the light years. But he knew it wasn't like that at all. In terms of conventional space-time, the suspended animation units now en route to Jamestown simply did not exist. They and their contents were now what the sub-space physicists called molecular echoes and they were in a continuum which, apparently, could only be defined mathematically.

Anyway, the important thing was that the matter receiver was functioning, the instrumentation showed that it would presently be operative, and all was ready for reception.

With the exception of Andreas all the Expendables were present, as were the robots Matthew and Mark. It was an occasion.

The matter receiver was a large steel box with one massive door capable of being vacuum-sealed. It had its own built-in atomic generator to produce the immense voltages for the receiving field.

There was a sudden hiss as all air was pumped out of the reception chamber.

"Reception sequence one, commencing," said Matthew. "All systems normal . . . Molecular echoes now matching pattern equation . . . Acceptance sequence commencing. All systems normal. Physical resolution now commencing. All systems normal."

Conrad gazed at the matter receiver, fascinated, though there was nothing yet to be seen. But inside that enigmatic black box a miracle was taking place. Matter —steel, flesh, bone, blood—that had leaped the light years as a colossal but insubstantial and controlled blast of sub-spatial radiation was now returning to its normal form. Conrad was reminded of the saying of some ancient Terran philosopher: What man has imagined and desired, that he will ultimately achieve.

Lieutenant Smith shivered. "I feel as if we are in the presence of ghosts."

Kwango laughed: "These ghosts will live and breed more ghosts. Pretty damn soon, there will be a population problem."

Fidel said: "Kurt—as our esteemed brother Lou would have put it—you are full of colonic verbalese."

Chantana gave a faint smile. "As an ecologist, Kurt, you should know that it will take a thousand years before Kratos has any population problems. Maybe by then mankind will have acquired a little wisdom."

"Physical resolution completed," said Matthew. "All systems normal. Unit one ready for disposal. Instructions required."

"Open up," said Conrad. "Wheel it out."

"Decision noted," said Matthew imperturbably. "Execution proceeds."

There was a further hiss as air was readmitted to the chamber. Matthew pressed the button that released the vacuum seal. The door of the matter receiver opened.

Mark entered the chamber and pulled out a titanium cylinder, smoothly rounded at each end like a vast Mexican jumping bean. The cylinder slid out noiselessly on its built-in rollers.

Stencilled in large letters on the side of the cylinder was the word: Doctor. Underneath that in small lettering were the words: John K. Howard, aged twenty-nine, I.Q. 175, specialist tropical diseases, U.S. citizen.

"Welcome to Kratos," said Conrad to the cylinder. He turned to Mark. "Wheel him away to storage."

"Decision noted, Commander. Execution proceeds."

Matthew said: "Permission requested to recommence reception cycle."

"Permission granted."

"Decision noted. Execution proceeds."

The next one came out of the matter receiver seven minutes later.

The legend read in large letters: Geologist. In small letters: Mikhail Subakow, aged thirty-one, I.Q. 164, specialist seismology; Russian citizen.

"Welcome, Mikhail Subakow," said Conrad. "Wheel him away."

And so it went on through the long afternoon and into the night, with electric lights shining in Andreas Square, and with the robots indefatigably carrying out their duties.

The colonists came from all parts of Earth—probably as a deliberate result of U.N. policy.

Biologist: Greta Bergman, age twenty-seven, I.Q. 181, Swedish citizen.

Engineer: Jean-Baptiste Girdo, age thirty-four, I.Q. 133, French citizen.

Teacher: Flora Makinnon, I.Q. 128, Scottish citizen.

Psychologist: Mohan das Gupta, I.Q. 155, Indian citizen.

And so it went on . . . Scientists, engineers, technologists, teachers farmers, doctors—men and women with the skills that would be needed to build a human civilisation on the fertile world of Kratos . . .

It was almost daybreak before the last of the titanium cylinders had come out of the matter receiver. Matthew and Mark, needing no rest, had continued their work with absolute precision. Conrad, feeling ir-

rationally that his presence might be needed, had
stayed by the matter receiver until more than seventy
colonists had arrived safely and been transferred to the
storage chamber. Then he had returned to the *Santa
Maria* and slept restlessly for a couple of hours.

Now, as the last colonists were arriving, here he was
once more, watching Matthew check the reception se-
quences with unwavering efficiency. He glanced up.
Soon the lights could be switched off. The sky was already grey and the stars were winking out, one by one.

"Physical resolution completed," said Matthew.
"Unit one hundred received. All systems normal."

"All systems normal," echoed Conrad. He smiled.
The phrase seemed, somehow, absurd. He had just
witnessed the completion of a scientific and technical
miracle. He felt privileged. He was in at the beginning
of man's colonisation of the first extra-solar world.
Privileged and humble . . . All systems normal . . .

"Permission requested to shut down matter receiver,
Commander."

"Permission granted."

"Decision noted. Execution proceeds."

"Permission requested to watch the dawn of a new
day on Kratos, Commander." It was not the voice of
Matthew. Conrad knew whose voice it was.

He turned and saw Lieutenant Smith standing a little
behind him. She looked tired—tired and beautiful.

"Permission granted."

Indira smiled and stepped forward. "Decision noted.
Execution proceeds."

Conrad held her hand, remembering when he had
first held it, more than 1 K-year ago.

"You have a heavy resuscitation programme ahead

of you, Indira. Can you and Matthew bring ten out tomorrow—I mean today? I'll schedule the priorities, and we'll all help."

Indira sighed. "You are a hard man, James."

He grinned. "The sooner we get them out and give them their basic orientation, the sooner we can get ourselves put down and return to Earth."

"Why are you in such a hurry?"

"Two reasons. The first is that I am impatient to get the top brain surgeons working on Lou. The second is that we shall all get a long leave. I thought of spending most of it on Terra at a place called Applecross in the North-West Highlands of Scotland . . ." His grip on her hand tightened. "I thought—foolishly perhaps—that you might like to see Applecross, too."

"My tin legs don't bother you?"

He touched his silver eye patch. "Does that bother you?"

"No."

"Or my tin arm?"

Indira shook her head. "Tell me about Applecross," she said. "Look, the sun is rising . . . Look at those wonderful streaks of crimson in the sky."

"It will be even more wonderful in the Scottish Highlands," predicted Conrad.

"Then I had better go with you, Commander, if only to see if you are telling the truth."

"Decision noted, Lieutenant. Execution proceeds."

Addendum

Conrad, James. Ex-commander U.N.S.S., Commander Expendables, Team One. Age 37. Nationality British. Awarded Grand Cross of Gagarin for services rendered on Kratos. Offered reinstatement in U.N.S.S. with restored rank of captain. Offer declined. Elects to remain Expendable.

Smith, Indira. Ex-surgeon lieutenant, Terran Disaster Corps. Second-in-Command, Expendables, Team One. Age 29. Nationality Indian. Awarded D.S.S.C. for services rendered on Kratos. Offered rank of captain in Terran Disaster Corps. Offer declined. Elects to remain Expendable.

Kwango, Kurt. Ecologist, felon. Age 32. Nationality Nigerian. Granted free pardon for crimes committed. Awarded U.N. Gold Medallion for services rendered on Kratos. Offered Chair of Ecology, Syrtis University, Mars. Offer declined. Elects to remain Expendable.

Andreas, Lou. Engineer. Age 37. Nationality American. Awarded U.N. Silver Medallion for services rendered on Kratos and the Solar Cross for injuries received in the course of duty. Discharged with honour, unfit for further service.

Le Gros, Chantana. Scientist, felon. Age 28. Nationality Vietnamese. Granted free pardon for crimes committed. Awarded U.N. Silver Medallion for services rendered on Kratos. Offered Chair of Extra-terrestrial Chemistry, Brisbane University, Terra. Offer declined. Elects to remain Expendable.

Batista, Fidel. Weapons and explosive expert, felon. Age 31. Nationality Cuban. Granted free pardon for crimes committed. Awarded U.N. Silver Medallion for services rendered on Kratos. Offered post as Advisor on Weaponry, U.N. Extra-Solar Division Offer declined. Elects to remain Expendable.

James, Elizabeth. Biologist, felon. Age 26. Nationality Welsh. Posthumously granted free pardon for crimes committed. Posthumously awarded U.N. Silver Medallion for services rendered on Kratos.

FILE CLOSED

From Fawcett Gold Medal . . .

Great Adventures in Reading

Fiction

SLAVES OF SABREHILL   X3304 $1.75
by Raymond Giles

Non-Fiction

ANN LANDERS SPEAKS OUT   Q3305 $1.50
by Ann Landers

Science Fiction

THE DEATHWORMS OF KRATOS   P3306 $1.25
by Richard Avery

THE RINGS OF TANTALUS   P3307 $1.25
by Richard Avery

Romance

TO SEEK A STAR   M3308   95¢
by Suzanne Ebel

DEAR TOM   M3309   95¢
by Jane Fraser

Cartoon

I CAN'T UNTIE MY SHOES   M3310   95¢
by Bil Keane

FAWCETT

Wherever Paperbacks Are Sold